BETTER THAN WAR

FLANNERY
O'CONNOR
AWARD
FOR
SHORT
FICTION

Nancy Zafris,
Series Editor

BETTER THAN WAR

STORIES BY
SIAMAK VOSSOUGHI

THE UNIVERSITY OF

GEORGIA PRESS

ATHENS AND

LONDON

© 2015 by the University of Georgia Press
Athens, Georgia 30602
www.ugapress.org
Designed by Kaelin Chappell Broaddus
Set in 9.5/14 Quadraat OT by Kaelin Chappell Broaddus
Printed and bound by Sheridan Books, Inc.
The paper in this book meets the guidelines for
permanence and durability of the Committee on
Production Guidelines for Book Longevity of the
Council on Library Resources.

Most University of Georgia Press titles are
available from popular e-book vendors.

Printed in the United States of America
19 18 17 16 15 C 5 4 3 2 1

Library of Congress Cataloging-in-Publication Data
Vossoughi, Siamak.
[Short stories. Selections]
Better than war : stories / by Siamak Vossoughi.
    pages cm. — (Flannery O'Connor Award for Short Fiction)
ISBN 978-0-8203-4853-7 (hardcover : alk. paper) —
ISBN 978-0-8203-4852-0 (ebook)   1. Iranian Americans—
Fiction.   2. Alienation (Social psychology)—Fiction.
3. Assimilation (Sociology)—Fiction.   I. Title.
PS3622.O88A6 2015
813'.6—dc23

                                        2015002100

British Library Cataloging-in-Publication Data available

For Majid and Nahid and Shirin

Dream the dreams of other men.

—PEARL JAM

CONTENTS

ACKNOWLEDGMENTS

Some of these stories were originally published, sometimes in slightly different form, in the following publications: "Nine Innings" in *River and Sound Review* (Spring 2012); "The Movie Quitters" in *Fourteen Hills* 18.2 (2012); "The Easel" in *Black Heart Magazine* (November 2013); "The World Is My Home" in *Sundog Lit* (September 2014); "Take Our Daughters to Work Day" in B|*Ta'arof* (October 2012); "Why the Rabbit Looks Pityingly Upon the Donkey" in *Cease, Cows* (April 2012); "The Narrator" in *The Brooklyn Voice* (October 2013); "The Book That Was Too Good to Read" in *Prick of the Spindle* (April 2012); "Shoes" in *Kenyon Review Online* (Winter 2015); People in Profile in *Missouri Review* (Winter 2014); "Back and Forth" in *Bellingham Review* (Spring 2015).

Thank you to the Flannery O'Connor Award Committee:

Nancy Zafris
Frank Soos
Amina Gautier
Dawna Kemper
Antara Brewer
L. Rebecca Harris

BETTER THAN WAR

SHOES

Hossein Mirzazadeh needed new shoes. The buying of the shoes themselves was a good adventure. He drove into downtown Seattle during his lunch break. There was a place that sold department-store items at a reduced price. The bustle of cities still made him think of Tehran, though it had been twenty-five years since he'd lived there. It was good to be a part of it. He could move within that city rhythm with familiarity.

The shoes were black, simple, similar to the ones he had. As a boy he would get new shoes once a year, at Nowruz. It was about the same now. It was good for a man to buy shoes, he felt. They served a very good purpose. They would be the shoes he saw when he woke up in the morning, the ones he placed in a locker when he went swimming at the pool, and the ones he would put away in his closet at night.

He put the shoes in the trunk of his car. On the way back to his office he thought of a young man he'd known in Iran who hadn't come to one of their political meetings because he was wearing new shoes. The meetings were up in the mountains. The young man had not wanted to get his shoes scuffed. We are trying to make a society where you'll have a lot more to care about than your shoes, Hossein had told him. Of course we have to go up in the mountains to talk like that. Hossein had known that they were the young man's only pair. But all of them who were going up there had only one pair. That was why they were all going up there together, while women in the Shah's family were flying to Paris for a day to buy shoes.

Hossein still remembered the sight of the young man turning around and walking away. He'd told the others that in the Iran they were going to build, people were not going to care so much about material possessions. But he'd felt miserable that he hadn't been able to reach the part of the young man that cared more about justice than shoes. Each time he was able to bring another person along when they went up to the mountains—a student, one of the men he'd been in the army with—the revolution succeeded, and so with the young man who didn't want to get his shoes scuffed, he'd wondered if the revolution had failed. He'd wondered as they'd hiked up, and then it was like a lot of things—he'd put it out of his mind when it was time to put it out of his mind.

Coming home from work that day, Hossein believed himself to be a lucky man. There are men you can't describe without starting with their hope for their people. You'll start describing their hair color or eye color or style of dress, and you'll think, What does this have to do with them? What does this have to do with the look in their eye as they're walking down the street, the way that a universe is being filtered through another day of striving, a striving that is not just their striving but their people's striving? Hossein's notion of his own good fortune had to do with the way he had found some ways to keep that hope alive in him despite being here in America and despite everything that had gone wrong in Iran.

He left the shoes in the trunk of his car and came in with a glad and excited feeling to see his family. They were all wonderful people. The smell of his wife's cooking filled the house and eased his mind. His son was reading the paper with a beautiful serious look on his face. His daughter was talking on the phone and laughing. A family was what a man got instead of a revolution, though it was better to think that they were what he got along with a revolution. He was proud that each of them carried a hope for revolution inside them as well. It gave a liveliness to their house that came through when they sat down together in the evening, with somebody usually laughing so hard that they had to get up to walk around. It was the truth that was the funniest thing in the world. Hossein didn't know exactly when he had discovered that, but it was a good principle because it meant a man didn't try to be funny unless he had something to say.

And dinner gave him a chance to do the other thing he was very good at, which was to eat. Nobody really knew how he did it, but somehow in the first five minutes his plate was nearly clean. And when it was clean, it was clean. No stray grain of rice or bit of chicken remained—only the cooked tomato skins that did not go down well. When he ate particularly fast, his wife would chastise him.

Have you ever been through a famine? Hossein would say. If you had lived through a famine like I did when I was seven, you would eat fast too.

His children would laugh, and he appreciated how they would laugh each time even though the joke was familiar. Underneath their laughter was a respect for famine.

Underneath everything was a respect for everything. If a family was what a man got instead of a revolution, at least the life of his family carried some of the same principles that he had hoped would run the life of his people. Nobody placed himself above anybody else. Nobody saw a big piece of chicken at the table and tried to take it for himself. It was important because he had seen those men. He had seen men who were given the small piece of chicken at work and took the big piece at home. At some point it had become too much to see it everywhere, starting from the top and trickling downward, and he had left. Since then, he had seen that it had more to do with the world than with Iran, but that was something that he had had to see for himself.

What he was interested in now was the way a family could be a place to go with those feelings. His son and his daughter wanted very much to hear stories of Iran and political work and prison. And they happened to be who he wanted to tell. He could tell them in the way he wanted to tell them, which was that there was a part of the story that was over and done, and there was a part of it that was still going. It was easy to do when the listeners themselves were very much just starting out and still going. And he didn't tell them with the expectation that they should follow in his path. He had too much faith in his path. And he had too much faith in his children too; they were already listening to understand themselves.

He didn't know that he had been looking for a listener for all that stuff. When he thought of the men who had died, it made the most sense to keep it inside him, where the memory of those men would stay true. But there were people in the world you could tell about things like that and nothing happened to the memory when it came out. Or if anything did happen, it was something confirming, because the people listening would start with silence and usually end with silence. There were at least two people like that in the world.

And that was more than he had expected, because the world had not stopped when those men had died. It had kept on expecting and demanding, and there had been a younger brother and sister to take care of, and a mother to support, and jobs and jobs, at day and at night, and then a wife of his own, and leaving the country, and starting all over again in America, and then the same two children who sat before him listening. He felt twenty-five sometimes when he told them about those days, and he looked it as well. His children could see who he had been at twenty-five more clearly than they could from old photographs. It was an aliveness in him, whose excess they had always felt in the way it could go in any direction that life gave him, watching and learning about baseball with his son, joking with his daughter's American friends, but this was the basic soul of it, where it all came from, and they were humbled to see that where that aliveness came from was death and that it came unassumingly from death, from the same man who watched and learned baseball with them and who joked with their friends. And even the way they were humbled was nothing he would bask in, not even as a storyteller noticing his effect, because really the main part of the story was the part that was still going, for all the love he had for those men, he made a listener feel as if the important part of the story was the part that was still going, because his point in telling it was not to take but to give. It was when he told them of what was over and done that he realized himself how much of it was still going.

And it was still going that night when he drank a glass of water just before going to bed. The water woke him up at two o'clock in the morning, as he had expected it to, and he got out of bed to use the bathroom. Then he went to the garage. He opened the trunk of his car and took out the shoes. He was not the kind of man who would come home carrying new shoes he had bought for himself. He had needed them, and he had bought them, but they were just shoes. There were some other things he wanted to carry coming home to his family, and they were harder to hold. If he had to not hold on to his shoes in order to come in carrying them, that was all right. If he had to go and get them from his car in the middle of the night, that was nothing but a way to remember what shoes really were, which was something that everybody deserved to have.

THE BROKEN FINGER

One of the men who set my course in life was someone I did not know. He was a man my father knew in the Shah's prison in Iran. He was having his finger pulled back by one of his jailers when he said, "If you pull it back any farther, it will break." They pulled it, and it broke.

"You see now," he said. "I told you it would break."

As a boy, all I saw was the courage and the sense of purpose. I wanted to have something that could look at a broken finger like that. The closest I could come was scraping up my knees when I tried to ride my bike down impossible hills. My father hated to see it. He had seen enough of men and boys beaten and bloodied. It was no part of his intention in having a boy to see it in him. Still, he would tell those stories. And pretty soon I would find myself on my bike at the top of another hill, and I would think, It's the least I can do—it's the least I can do to try to go down this hill. It was a question of scale. A man in prison spoke calmly to the men who were breaking his finger, and a boy at the top of a hill rode down it.

When I got older, I saw that the man my father knew in prison had had his eye on something in the distance. The men who stood between him and that thing were deserving of the truth, nothing more and nothing less. They did not block his vision. They did not interrupt what his vision told him about life. A broken finger had not been part of it, but his vision was big enough that it could fit in it. What I saw was that the work of speaking calmly about a broken finger came before a broken finger. You had to dig deeper in yourself, but you had to dig deeper in yourself and in nobody else. The man in prison had made his prison cell the world. It seemed so easy. It was a crazy thing to say, but sometimes it seemed so easy. It was what the men who broke his finger did that seemed hard.

The whole thing was a happy story. To a boy of eight, it was the story of how much a man could do in the world. I didn't think of the men who did the breaking as men. I didn't think of them as something a boy could grow up to be. In my imagination, those men had never been boys. The point where life became hard was the point when I realized that those men *had* been boys.

It didn't come to me at once. It came to me in pieces. But those pieces came together in a small apartment in the middle of a big American city, and I looked out the window, and I saw everybody in the light of that prison cell. What if you felt like crying not for your broken finger but for the boys those men had been? What did you do then? What if the world figured that you were crying for yourself and you didn't feel the urge to tell it otherwise?

And I thought that maybe the man with the broken finger did have his eye on something in the distance, but he had his eye on something very near too. He had his eye on his jailers, on who they were and on who they had been. It was so near that he saw more of them than they knew. They didn't know that they were worthy of being spoken to calmly by a man whose finger they had broken, but they were.

I looked out the window, and I said to everybody, I don't want to tell you about yourself as if it's something you don't know. I just want to be there for you at a certain moment, at the moment of the broken finger. It was always the moment of the broken finger. It was always that moment, and the same thing that made a boy feel glad to be part of this whole thing made a young man wonder if he could.

What saved me were words. It was still the man with the broken finger. He had used words to say that he was in charge of his own story. I wanted to do the same thing. The thing about words was that a couple of true ones were as big as millions of them that didn't know themselves. It was what went into the words. It was the way they were earned. The man with the broken finger had earned the right to tell his jailers that he had told them so. With something smaller, he might've let it go. He might've let generosity take over. But a broken finger was an ordeal, and he had told them that it would happen. They ought to know so that next time they were doing that, they would listen to the man whose finger they were pulling.

I wanted to write like that. I wanted to write as though next time they would listen to the man whose finger they were pulling. It was completely crazy, but it was completely practical too. I wanted to say that it was always a couple of people in a room, but it was always the world stage too. The question was how did the people live up to that, and the answer was that they already did, and it was my job as a writer to prove it.

THE STREET

The street: For some the street is a way to get to a place and for some it is a place. But it *is* a place. All it takes for a place is for a man to stop. The question is, who stops on a street? Where I lived it was beggars and writers. They were both stopping to ask for something, and what they were asking for was similar. Sometimes a beggar would ask a writer, and the writer would look at him because he was interested in a fellow asker. Sometimes a writer would ask a beggar, only with less directness. Or more directness, depending. It didn't seem like there could be anything more direct than an empty stomach, but sometimes it could seem like there was. Nothing was as good as food for an empty stomach, but that wasn't always the only emptiness. Those writers whose fathers had been revolutionaries who had told them about hunger strikes knew somewhere inside them that an empty stomach was no match for a full heart.

That was another time when the street was a place, when people gathered to say that nobody should be a beggar and everybody should be a writer, at least in terms of writing his or her own story. That was why the writers were always stopping: walking past and not stopping was somebody else's story. They didn't know exactly whose, but it wasn't their own. Until a man had learned to see the street as a place, he was operating under the conditions of somebody else's story. Until he had seen it like that, he had not seen himself.

That was the thing about destinations—they had a way of clearing up all that uncertainty, of making a man feel as if he knew himself through and through, so much so that he could start feeling it on the way there, and he wouldn't have to see the street at all. It was the beggars and writers for whom a destination wasn't enough. There was an emptiness, either of a stomach or a heart, and if they didn't get it straightened out right there on the street, it was going to be with them when they got to their destination, wherever they were going. There was no choice but to look at the street and to see it as a place, because it was as likely as any place to be where they got it straightened out, where that emptiness was made, at least a little and at least for that day, full.

There were people there, that was a start, but they looked like they had far different concerns from those of the beggars and writers. The matters of a stomach and a heart looked like things they had figured out a long time ago. It was breathtaking to see the ease with which they seemed to handle them. The beggars and writers wondered if the people had ever been hungry. Everyone they saw seemed to have a little bit of it, but what they were wondering about was that absolute hunger, that hunger with nowhere to go because hunger was going to be there whether they went to place A or place B, so there was nothing to do but to sit.

Energy was being conserved at least when they sat, and it would come in useful the next time they were walking. When a man made a decision to sit in a street, whether it was with a cup or with a pen and paper, he was making a commitment to the street as a place, a place where his intention was to survive. He had a love for a place like that, however hungry he was and however far away everybody else's concerns were. This place can help me, he thought, if I can get down under it, if I can get inside it, if I can prove to everybody that it is a place, that just because you're walking doesn't mean that all the love and beauty and sorrow is reserved for coming out only at the place you're trying to get to. All that stuff isn't temporarily on hold walking down a city street. If it was, I wouldn't see it so clearly.

That was what he was after, even more than quarters and stories. If he could get that, the quarters and stories would come. He was asking the street to be what it could be, and in a way he was saying that he would return the favor. Okay, street—me and you. I don't know how, but somehow or another: me and you. One of the things a man did when he sat in a street was face its people, and in facing them, he was saying that he was not going to take them for granted. He was not going to act like there was anything of theirs with which he was going to take liberties.

It was a way of meeting that hunger that could seem like the slower way. There was another way that could seem like the faster way. It involved a man saying to the world that he already knew it, that the street was not something he was under, but over. Its people were defined by what they were to him, and if they did not seem to share his hunger, that was all he needed to know to dismiss their rights to their quarters and their stories. That was how fierce his hunger was, that he could look at all of it and say: For what? For what all this acting like there was love and beauty and sorrow in the world when a man was hungry? For what acting like he was any different from everybody around him if he were to take without asking?

Something about the street would not let him do it, though. It was the way that people became a one-at-a-time thing when a man stopped, and one at a time, it made sense to ask. It made sense to look at each one of them and say, I don't know. I don't know anything except that you are worth asking, that what you could give me is something worth asking for. It wouldn't even be what it was if it was taken without asking. Quarters taken without asking would not lead to a sandwich eaten in peace, and stories written like that would not lead to any peace either. A beggar and a writer were exercising greatness in not taking, in handing their fate over to time. A man had to choose between being under and being over, and under was the only place he could ask from.

What happened then was that he learned to take some of that asking with him when he was walking. It was something he could take with him anywhere. There was something that stayed still as he was moving. It was something that had to do with his concern for the placeness of where he was more than where he was going. If a man was smart about his hunger, he knew that it was never really met, and so there was no point in thinking of when it had been or dreaming of when it would be. All a man had was the place in front of him, and if there were things he wanted to tell the people while he was there, all he could do was remember to tell them with asking, with the spirit of asking, which was the spirit of the people themselves, who were asking the same question: Is there love and beauty and sorrow in the world?

The beggars and writers where I lived were stating things by doing their asking aloud, by sitting in the street and doing it up front and out in the open, for all to see. They were stating that it was a good place to do it, for one thing. They were stating that they could not wait a while and take it as an article of faith later on that the answer was yes, neither could they take it as such that it was no. Faith was a nice thing, but the question was too earthly for that. It had the earthliness that needed answering where it was hardest to find it. The only faith was that somehow the cause of their hunger contained its alleviation in it. Their hunger had given them a chance to see just how much of a place the street was, and in a way they were thankful for that. It wouldn't be good to have walked down the street for years and then finally see that it was a place itself. There would be a lot that would've been missed. The beggars and writers told themselves that if they were ever lucky enough to have destinations, they wouldn't start missing the street itself on the way there. They told themselves that even if it were the best destination, the place where love and beauty and sorrow could be found in perfect measure, they wouldn't start missing even the smallest part of the street. If anything, they would start seeing even more of it, because that was the place where they could afford to walk to slowly and take their time. They wouldn't have to have any rush to it, because that was where they always knew they were going anyway.

NINE INNINGS

She was in New York and I was in San Francisco, and I was getting better at not thinking about her each day, but on TV at Nick's the Giants were playing the Mets, which meant that I could see that something in San Francisco could touch something in New York, and it was not me touching her, but still it was possible, a guy could get on a plane, and a little while later he'd be in New York, not at a ballpark but at a woman's apartment, and so I told myself, Okay, you've got nine innings, then let it go.

By the seventh, it was 16–2 Mets.

"Lousy game," the guy next to me said.

"In what sense?" I said.

In the eighth the bartender made a move to change the channel.

"No," I said.

"We're getting killed."

"There is a woman I love in New York," I said.

"Is she at the game?"

"No. She doesn't like baseball."

"If she was at the game, that would be one thing," the guy next to me said.

"She's in the city. She's going to see all these people tomorrow."

It was true. She was going to see all of them tomorrow, and I was going to see everybody in San Francisco tomorrow, and they were all perfectly nice people to see, but none of them would be her. Those fellows understood. They understood even if they didn't know it just then.

I saw another fellow at the end of the bar seem to ask the bartender to change it, and the bartender nodded toward me. I can tell you the whole story if you want, I thought. I can tell you how we knew each other in college, and somehow we both knew that if I ever felt the world steadily enough under my own two feet, it would be love. It had been love back then too, except I only had declarations and dramatic gestures to offer her back then, not the easy and sure understanding of what life was and how love fit into it, rather than the other way around. I'd thought of myself as an expert on love back then and a beginner at life, and I tried not to think about expertise at all these days, but the other way around was a good place to start at least.

So when we saw each other back home in Seattle at Christmas, and she saw what had fallen away from me and what was left, we picked up right where I had always wished we'd left off.

In the ninth, Pablo Sandoval hit a three-run home run. I didn't say a word. 16–5 was nothing to get excited about. The fellows at the bar took on the look of old hands, knowing that only someone who was some kind of beginner at baseball would think there was a chance.

But the Giants put a couple of hits together, a single and two doubles, and it was 16–7. Nine runs was still an impossibility. But I saw the fellow at the end of the bar staring intently at his beer, as if in reconsideration of something. A walk followed, and then Andres Torres hit a three-run shot. 16–10. I saw the fellow get up and walk toward me.

"I hope you see her soon," he said.

"Thank you," I said.

"I did not want to watch the game anymore. When they said you'd asked to leave it on because of a woman in New York, I thought that was foolish. I am sorry for thinking that."

"It's all right," I said. "16–2 is a blowout."

"Yes, it is. But I should show a little more faith. Whatever happens now, I should show a little more faith."

We watched as Freddy Sanchez hit a double.

"I hope you see her too," the guy next to me said. "She must be something," he said, as if she was the one standing on second base.

"She is."

She would've liked these two guys. She liked people and their funny old ways. She was like me—she got angry about people, and she loved them, and she tried to lean a little more to the part of her that loved them. That was what was so nice about seeing each other in Seattle, that we saw how hard each of us had been working since college, and love was seeing the possibility at least of someone you didn't have to work your hardest around. It was almost too much to look at, for me.

Buster Posey hit a bloop to right that fell in, so it was men on first and third, one out. When Pablo hit a double, the place went crazy.

"Listen," the fellow from the end of the bar said. "You need to get on a plane and go to New York."

"That's nice of you to say."

"Forget nice. We're watching this because of her. If she can do this all the way in New York, imagine what she can do when you're in the same place."

"She can do more than this," I said.

"That is what I am saying."

There was a strikeout, but along the way there was a wild pitch and Pablo made it to third. Then Mike Fontenot singled him home. 16–13.

"If we win this," the guy said, "I'm going to help buy your ticket. That's all there is to it. You have to go."

Men can get drunk in all kinds of ways, and one of them is witnessing the greatest sobriety of others. The Giants looked as sober as I had ever seen them, but every man in the bar was drunk. They'd gone somewhere they didn't think they could go. Nobody knew that when it came to drunkenness, I'd had to set up some rules since the last time I saw her: three drinks if the music being played didn't make me think of her, two drinks if it did.

"I'll help out too," the other guy said.

It was beautiful. They wanted to do something like the Giants were doing on TV. They wanted to exceed something. I thought I might just have to give them the chance.

Aaron Rowand was up. I watched the ball leave his bat on the second pitch. I smiled. Maybe I really would see her. He didn't hit many out, but when he did, you knew it off the bat.

Everybody embraced. It was a magnificent moment. She had done it. She had done it without even trying, which was how she did everything. That and trying very hard.

I had to remember that we were still down by a run. But I felt like I had won because everybody believed me that there was a woman in New York I loved.

"If you don't go now," the first guy said. "I am going to be upset."

"I certainly don't want to make you upset."

"No, you don't. You need to go and tell her about this. Thirteen runs in an inning. In the ninth."

"I'll try. But she doesn't know much about baseball."

"This isn't baseball. It's more than that."

"What is it?"

"Love."

It was good to hear someone else say it. We didn't have a street we could walk down together or a bar we could sit in together, but there was a guy in San Francisco who could see it, having seen the Giants score thirteen runs in the ninth.

The next batter struck out. I don't want to say his name because it was too heartbreaking.

"Still," the fellow from the end of the bar said, "your point is made."

The game was over, and everybody was wondering what to do next. I wanted very much to stay moving. I stood up to leave.

"Everything I said is still true," the fellow said. "She is the one for you."

"Thanks," I said.

"You'll go to New York, right?"

"I'll go."

He smiled. The game was ending with a little bit of fittingness and rhythm for him at least as long as I would go to New York.

And I would. I would go sometime. I just wouldn't go because of the ninth inning, even if the Giants had come all the way back and won. I would go because of the game, because of the way the people had looked back in the second inning, just to be in the same city as her. I would go because of something that wasn't desperate and dramatic but sure and easy, the kind of sureness and ease that had all kinds of hardship inside it that I didn't have to tell anybody about, that I didn't have to tell *her* about at least, because she just knew. She knew what it took for me to watch a game in San Francisco that was being played in New York, and in that sense she knew baseball as well as anybody at the bar.

I could be wrong, I thought, but I don't think there's a clock to this thing. She was in New York, and I was in San Francisco, but somehow we had already won. There was more than the ninth inning to baseball, and there was more than a plane flight across the country to love.

Still, I thought I'd stay away from Nick's for a while. It had been awfully nice to have that guy root for me and her back there, and I liked the thought of him keeping that up.

THE MOVIE QUITTERS

The movie was wonderful, beautiful, heartbreaking.

"The hell with this," my uncle said. "I'm tired of being moved to tears by American movies. When are Americans going to be moved to tears by Iranian movies? It's no good."

He wiped his eyes. "I've had it. I've had it with their joys and sorrows and their music in the background. It is too beautiful. I do not have the room inside myself anymore. I have seen too much."

"It was a good movie," my aunt said.

"Of course it was a good movie. That's the whole problem. William," my uncle said to my cousin Niloufar's husband William, "when are your parents coming to visit?"

"Three weeks."

"Okay. When your parents come to visit, we are going to watch a sad and beautiful Iranian movie. I am sorry. It has come to this. Look at me. I am crying. I am crying over an American movie. I am not going to feel good until I see an American man crying over an Iranian movie."

"What about an American woman crying?" my cousin said.

"That will help. But a man understands another man's tears."

"That is a man for you," my aunt said. "Even when there is something that you do not do as freely, you think there's something special when you do it."

"I did not say that it is special. I said that I understand it."

"But the underlying point is that women cry too easily."

"I am not smart enough to have underlying points. If I knew about underlying points, I would've noticed what all these American movies are doing to me."

"What?" I said.

"They are making me nostalgic for memories I don't even have. They are making me remember things I don't even know. 'Ah yes, good old America in the 1950s.' It is ridiculous. What the hell do I know about America in the 1950s?"

"Isn't that the point of a good movie," my cousin said, "to make you feel like you are inside it?"

"Yes, of course," my uncle said. "That is why I am crying. But it is not a two-way street. It is not a free and open exchange. I am through. For my part I am through. Until I see an American man or woman cry over an Iranian movie, I am done with them."

Over the next three weeks my uncle read seventeen books. He told me about them when I came to visit.

"Did you know that there are more sheep than people in New Zealand?" he said.

"Yes," I said.

"I have been sticking to it. No movies. I have been remembering myself."

"That's good," I said.

"Yes," he said. "Come on. Let's go to the video store. William's parents are coming tomorrow. We need to find a movie that is sad but not too sad. It shouldn't take our saddest movie to make them cry."

"I don't think there are any Iranian movies that are sad but not too sad."

We went to the Iranian video store in Bellevue. My uncle explained what he was looking for to Mr. Houshang, the owner.

"All movies are sad," Mr. Houshang said. "American or Iranian. Do you know why?"

No, we said.

"Because when we watch them, we see how hard we have been trying. Look at them. Look at how hard they have to work to make a movie. Look at how many people it takes. What is all that work for? It is to try to be us. Good God, we have been working hard."

He gave us a movie that he said was sad but not because of anybody young or beautiful dying.

"I think he is a wise man," I said when we left.

"Yes," my uncle said. "I was not prepared for that much wisdom. Maybe I have been thinking about this all wrong. I have been thinking of how much I have been giving of myself to American movies. I have not been thinking of what American movies have been giving me."

My uncle was quiet for a while.

"All right, all right," he said. "But is it a lot to ask for a two-way street? Is it a lot to say that I would like to see an American man cry as I have cried?"

"No," I said. "Or a woman."

"Or a woman," my uncle said.

The night that we watched the movie, I was trying very hard to not look at William's father and mother to see if an American man or woman would cry watching an Iranian movie. William's father did not seem like the kind of man who cried very often. He seemed like the kind of man who cried over a movie hardly ever. I thought my uncle was up against it. He was going to be reading books for a while.

The movie was wonderful and beautiful and heartbreaking. My uncle cried, and I did too. It was our country, and we missed it, and we didn't care what anybody else thought.

"The hell with it," my uncle said. "I am not watching any more Iranian movies. It is too sad."

It *was* too sad. I didn't like to think that there was a people just like us in every way except for everything about us that was from living in

America and everything about them that was from living in Iran. It didn't make any sense. I understood why my uncle had decided to quit watching American movies. It was a lot just to be from one place and watch the movies from there.

"I wish I knew how you felt," William's father said.

"What do you mean?" my uncle said.

"I would like to know how it feels to feel a movie is too sad," William's father said. "I have watched movies that are sad, but the movie ends, and I am back in the world."

"What is it like when you are there?" my uncle said.

"Where?"

"Back in the world."

"I don't know. It is the world. I have always been there."

"It is not the movie—it is the world," my uncle said to me that night after everybody had left. "It is like coming back from a trip and seeing where we live for the first time."

"Where do we live?"

"We live in America. But we also live everywhere we've ever been. We might also live in places we've never been. I don't know. Sometimes I suspect that that is the case. But the movie touches those parts, those parts that have lived everywhere. It is a very lucky thing to have lived in more than one place, Hamid. It is sad too, but in this world, it is a very lucky thing."

I couldn't explain it, but I knew that he was right. I thought that maybe I should give up movies too, if it meant understanding things like that.

IN THE LIBRARY

The two boys sat in the library after school. The newspaper on the table was opened to an article about their country. "Iran Sentences Woman to Death by Stoning," it said. They had read it. It was difficult to go straight to their chemistry homework after reading it.

"I don't remember hearing about stoning when we were still there," Mohammad Reza said.

"You were probably too young," Keyvan said.

"I was seven."

"You were probably too young."

"Well, somebody should have told me."

"What good would that have done?"

"I don't know."

The two boys had both covered their chemistry books in paper that was bright green, the color of the national protest movement. Sometimes it helped them to feel close to Iran. Other times they felt very far.

Some girls from their class were sitting at the next table. They were whispering excitedly about the upcoming school dance. Neither of the boys was going. They both had dreams of going. They hadn't told each other those dreams. They were very good friends, but they hadn't told each other those dreams.

"I would jump in front of her if I was there," Mohammad Reza said.

"They would shoot you."

Mohammad Reza shrugged. "I would do something."

"I would pick up a rock and pretend to miss and hit one of the people throwing a rock instead."

"Yes, that's it. Pretend to be the worst thrower in the world."

"It could be a distraction. You could get all the people in the crowd to throw rocks at each other instead."

It felt good to think of pretending to be bad throwers. They knew it wasn't going to feel good for long, but it was nice to imagine.

It was good to have somebody at school to be angry with. They each had a place to be angry at home too, but with each other they could be angry and funny and other things. There was another boy in their class who was Iranian, and they played basketball with him on weekends, but his family was royalist, and whenever he heard about something bad in Iran, he talked about America doing something to Iran about it.

"They believe that bombs can be messages of hope," Keyvan's father had told him about them. "I don't know why this is, but they believe it."

They watched the girls sitting at the next table. They hadn't told each other about their dreams of going to the dance, but that was partly because it was obvious. It would be a dance, and a girl in a dress, and arriving there together at night. What was there to tell? It would be a dream. If they were going to be angry about some things, it was good to have some things they dreamed of too.

The woman in the article had been convicted of killing her husband who had abused her. The boys knew how it was in Iran: women were supposed to be under men's control, even if the men were doing something like that. The way they were told it, it was not like that in America. The way they were told it, a woman could be anything she wanted to be. It did not make them feel better about anything. It did not make them feel better about being in America.

One of the girls at the next table had asked them once why they always read the newspaper. They hadn't understood her question. They thought she was asking why they didn't read a different newspaper. But she was asking why they read something that was so far away from them.

It was hard not to think after that that they wanted to go to the dance with a boy who did not read the newspaper. The two boys believed that they would want to know what was happening in Iran even if they weren't Iranian. It was because the dance was half the story. The other half was the world.

What was happening in the article was very far from them as they sat in the library, but they didn't think the idea was to call it very far from them. It was to call it very near to them and then to figure out how that was true. They threw themselves out to some place where they knew they didn't know what to do once they were there. But they thought that someday they could throw themselves out there, and they *would* know what to do there.

And it didn't matter if there were girls who did not want to go to the dance with a boy who read the newspaper. They had to be thinking of the woman in the article. They had to be thinking of what they owed her.

Just then their friend Alex came into the library. They waved, and he began walking to their table.

"Close the newspaper," Keyvan said.

"Why?"

"I don't like the way they read things like this. About women in Iran."

"What do you mean?"

"They read it to prove a point—to prove they are right about something. It is not the right way to read it."

Mohammad Reza closed the newspaper. Alex joined them, and after talking for a few minutes, they began to get to work on their chemistry homework.

TOO MUCH GENIUS

The boys took off running as Allie began to count. Each boy showed the kind of man he was and his general philosophy toward life by his approach toward hide-and-seek. Tom Pemberton ran straight to the tree and climbed to the top of it. The efficacy of the hiding place was secondary to the adventure of reaching it. If a hiding place was effective *and* difficult to reach, that was ideal, but the adventure came first.

Louie Parenti curled up under the bench on the side of the house. He was a boy of ten who stayed close to his five-year-old self in a number of ways, and squeezing into very small spots was one of them.

Sebby Dudum did not mind darkness. He found it soothing. He flipped a wheelbarrow upside down and went under it, prepared to sit there for as long as it took.

Jake Loewen ran behind a pile of firewood and lay back, looking up at the sky. It was an obvious place to look, but it was worth it to lay back and look up at the sky for a while. His mother and father were separating, and he wanted to make his time with his friends last as long as it could.

Romar Wilson ran to the front of the house. He was about to dive behind the hedges when he saw a car coming down the street that looked like that of his mother. He looked in the car and saw her. He turned to the house and waved good-bye to nobody. He walked casually over to the street as his mother pulled up.

"Did you thank Allie's mother?" his mother said.

"Yes."

"We have to stop at the market before we go home."

"Okay."

There are moments of genius in a man's life. There are moments when he feels that all his efforts have added up to something and he has become the person he has dreamed of becoming. Who am I? Romar thought in the backseat of his mother's car. Am I a great man, or am I mean and spiteful? Is it necessary to disregard other people in order to exercise genius? If there was a way to exercise it without disregarding them, I would prefer that. His father had told him that Einstein used to get so caught up in his scientific study that he would forget to put on pants. Maybe it was like that. Maybe some side effects couldn't be helped. He tried to think about how everybody would talk about it in the distant future: the day that Romar proved that he was the once-and-for-all champion of hide-and-seek. Not just the boys at Allie's house. The news would spread. It would go beyond the fifth grade. Fourth graders would be telling third graders about it. They would be talking about it even after he had left Fox Elementary and gone on to middle school.

"Did you have fun?" his mother said.

"Yes."

"What did you do?"

"We played football."

The problem with this kind of genius was not being able to talk about it. There was another kind that a guy could talk about, the kind that came with winning the class spelling bee, for example. But that was somebody else's idea of what constituted genius. It seemed like a man who pursued his own idea of it was always going to have to face loneliness.

Romar usually stayed in the car when his mother went to the market, but this time he came with her. It was better to be among the people and the noise and not dwell on his achievement. It *was* an achievement, though. How else was he supposed to achieve something? How else was he supposed to prove that life was more than just going to the market? He looked at the people examining fruits and vegetables, and he wondered if they knew how much they were capable of. They certainly didn't look as though they did. And he felt as if his achievement had not just been for himself; it had been to prove to everybody that there were great things that each person was capable of. It was a heavy burden for one man to have to carry, but he was used to that. At his school, where he was the only black boy in his class, there was a feeling that weighed on him in the classroom when they talked about Martin Luther King Jr. and the civil rights movement. He felt as if he was always expected to participate in the discussion, and sometimes he had something to say, and sometimes he didn't.

He looked around at the people in the market, and he thought that if he had to be the one to carry the burden of genius, then he would do it. The point of hide-and-seek was to hide, and he had hidden all right. There must have been a reason that his mother had come around the corner at just the right time. There must have been a reason he had been the only one to run to the front of the house and see her.

"Romar," his mother said. "They are out of the cereal that you like. We'll have to get corn flakes instead."

"No!" Romar said. Something collapsed inside him, and he thought of trying to carry the burden of genius without the cereal that he liked each morning, and it seemed like too much.

"What's the matter? You've had corn flakes before."

It was all of a piece—the cereal he liked and the championship of hide-and-seek and the way everyone at school would be proud of him.

He couldn't understand how something that had started out so beautifully could feel so bad. He began to cry. And he felt disappointed in himself because in the mornings when he sat eating the cereal he liked, he had sincerely believed that he was ready for the genius inside him.

When he told his mother what had happened, she gave him a furious look and said, "I'll decide on your punishment when we get home." She called Allie's mother and had Romar explain to her himself what he had done.

Allie's mother went outside and found the boys around the corner and halfway up the next block. They were looking underneath a parked car. She called to them that Romar had just called and he had already gone with his mother.

The boys walked back to the house in hushed respect. They were done with hide-and-seek for today and maybe forever. There was no point to it now. They didn't feel as if they had lost something, though. They felt as if they had gained something.

They sat on Allie's stoop. At that time, Romar was sitting in the backseat of his mother's car, eating a lollipop his mother had bought him because he'd felt so bad for what he'd done. The boys were each lost in the thought of imagining how it had happened. Tom Pemberton didn't think that climbing to the top of the tree in Allie's yard was much of a thing. Louie Parenti felt as if the world was much bigger than he knew. Sebby Dudum was imagining telling his father about it and how his father would turn quiet and thoughtful the way he had when Sebby's older brother had beaten him in chess. Jake Loewen smiled very happily. His mother and father were separating, and he cherished the time he could be away from home and with his friends. Romar's victory at hide-and-seek made him feel as if it all made sense, because the time with his friends was worth cherishing.

BETTER THAN WAR

I was thinking of an Iranian boy waiting to ask an American girl in his class out on a date because he wants to know first if there is going to be a war or not.

"What if we're at a movie theater together, and they make the announcement that the war has started, and the whole place whoops and hollers?"

"That would be terrible. Do you think she would whoop and holler with them?"

"No. I can't see it. She's too wonderful."

"That's good."

"But there's her family. What if her father is a marine sergeant who doesn't take any guff when it comes to questioning the chain of command?"

"Is that what he is?"

"No, he's an accountant. But it's the principle."

He was spooked. I understood it.

"Look," I said. "It makes sense. We're new to this."

"We're new to what? To living in a country that might start a war with the country we're from?"

"Yes," I said. "Here's what I think. I think you should ask her out on a date. If you go to a movie theater and they make an announcement that the war has started and the whole place whoops and hollers, I think you should cry if you feel like crying."

"Then where do we go from there?"

"You should go wherever you were planning on going."

"What if I just feel like taking her home?"

"Then you should take her home."

"What if her father comes out, and he's happy that the war has started, and I feel like fighting him?"

"You shouldn't fight him."

"Why not?"

"Because you're going to wake up the next day, and there's going to still be a war."

"But I'll feel better, won't I?"

"No, you won't. You'll feel worse."

He looked at me as if he was at least hoping I wouldn't say that.

"I hate war," he said.

"Me too."

"I'd hate it even if she weren't so pretty."

"I believe you."

"But it does make it easier to hate it."

"Maybe you and she could hate it together."

"I know. But sometimes that's not enough."

"When do you mean?"

"Sometimes how much I hate war is *all* I am."

"What do you do then?"

"I don't know. I try not to fight anybody."

"That's good."

"But if she sees me crying in a movie theater where they're whooping and hollering, she's going to want to know the whole story."

"It's good to tell *someone* the whole story."

"Yes, but what'll I have left?"

"You'll have a lot left."

"I will?"

"Yes, you'll have something no one's ever had left. An Iranian boy pouring his heart out to an American girl. You know what you'll have left? Your heart. You don't have to lose it when you pour it out."

"I don't?"

"No."

"Even if I cry in a movie theater?"

"Even if you cry at a puppet show. You don't think there are puppet shows in Iran? You don't think there are little kids watching them who deserve to watch them and who deserve to grow up and remember they watched them? You don't think they deserve a little peace? Crying is one of the most peaceful things you can do. If you hate war, you have to be a proponent of crying. Crying in a movie theater full of Americans while you're out with an American girl, that's some advanced-level crying. That's up in the treetops of crying. If they had any sense, they would join you. I hope to hell that *she* would join you."

"I think she would."

"Good."

"Sometimes I feel like crying just over the chance of a war."

"There's not a thing wrong with that. Makes all the sense in the world to me. I think if you cry over that, you should remember *how* you cry. And you should laugh like that. And you should eat like that. And you should tell her stories like that. You're going to have to be better than war."

"Better than war."

"Yes."

"I don't know if I can do it."

"You already know you hate it, don't you? That's the best part of hating something, is now you know what to be better than."

"The war is going to be everywhere."

"One boy can do it. One girl can do it."

"Do you think she can do it?"

"Yes. Do you?"

"Yes. She already is better than war to me."

"Maybe you are already better than war to her."

"That would be a good start. That would be a good start if I was better than war to her."

"And she would know that your crying is an effort to stay that way. And everything else."

"I hope someday I can be better than war without the need for any war."

"I hope you can do it too. I think that might be the whole point."

I don't know the Iranian boy or the American girl or the class they are in together. I guess it gets too hard to carry the possibility of war around by myself, so they rise out of me to make it a little easier. If I had a community of Iranians in America, with our own streets and neighborhoods and lazy afternoons, I guess they would rise out of that, but I don't, so they rise out of me instead. They're still just as real, and I still feel just as sorry for them, as much as if I could put down my pen and walk downstairs and go outside, and old Iranian men and women would be sitting in doorways and Iranian children playing and Iranian mothers and fathers calling for them to come inside, none of whom deserve to be waiting to hear about war before they can live, all of whom deserve every moment of life before them, knowing somewhere that each of them is better than war, and not needing any vision of war to remind them.

THE ROOM

Everybody was worried about Elham, but when they called Massoud at college and told him about it, he just laughed and laughed.

It was a good sign, he thought.

His poor mother and father. They had come to America hoping that their son and daughter would become doctors and lawyers. Now their son was studying Russian literature, and their daughter was fourteen, and her friends were seventeen- and eighteen-year-olds in recovery from drugs.

There was a little room next to the drug counselor's office at the high school, where those kids would go during the day. Elham spent her free time there. Their mother had spoken with the counselor, Ms. Devers. "Elham is not an addict, and she is not in recovery," Ms. Devers had said. "But she fits well in this space."

"What does it mean?" Massoud's mother asked. "I do not understand it. I do not want her to fit in that space."

As he listened, Massoud thought of the story in *Raise High the Roof Beam, Carpenters*, of the old Chinese horse expert who had become so attuned to the inner qualities of a horse that he would miss things like its color and its gender. He felt like the horse expert's friend, who was impressed at how instinctually his friend was feeling his way about the world.

It's not what they bargained for, he thought after he talked with them. It's not what they expected coming to this country. But this is the only country I've ever grown up in, and I know how it is when you are fourteen and you are crying for something real and decent. They ought to be happy she's found it. I guess they can't be expected to know it, but they ought to be happy about that.

You could throw yourself into your schoolwork, but a world was still happening around you, and Elham wasn't somebody who could look away from that, and neither should anybody want her to. The question was, where could you go in that world where life had a human pace, where people were looking at each other as though across an even divide, not looking up and not looking down? If the only place was the little room next to the drug counselor's office, that was a whole lot better than nothing.

Massoud remembered the place from when he was a student at the high school. He remembered walking by once and thinking that the kids in there were the least of his problems. They weren't putting their pain on anybody else. If anything, they were putting it on themselves. There was a boy he'd seen in there who was in his drama class, Todd Lucas. He was jittery, but that Todd Lucas could really listen. He was one of the best listeners Massoud had ever seen. It was as though he knew how lucky he was to be listening to anything.

If you wanted to be loose and easy about it, you could say that Americans who were in recovery from drugs were realizing something that Iranians knew all along. He laughed. Of course, that was only if you wanted to be loose and easy about it.

Well, he thought, at least one other person in the world knew how he felt.

It was a fine way to be fourteen. They ought to be glad that she was skipping drugs and going straight to recovery. But he knew he couldn't expect that. How could he tell them? Look, he thought, you can put your head down and put everything into your schoolwork, but it's not going to change the fact that there is a world out there, and its foolishness and carelessness can't just be dismissed, not if you want to make something beautiful out of it. Somehow you have to figure out what you're going to do about all of it, and that was what he wished they could see, that Elham had already started figuring, that she wasn't hiding from that, and there weren't a whole lot of options when you were fourteen, but a place where everybody was admitting by their presence there that life was a difficult thing and it took some purposefulness to live it correctly was, all things considered, a good start.

He felt bad for all of them, Elham and his mother and father and aunt and cousins, back there in his old town and nobody able to talk to each other.

They'd expect him to do something when he went home. They'd expect him to explain something, but he didn't know what he could do except to listen to everybody fairly, fairly enough that nobody would think he was taking sides, and his family might even have a wisp of a thought that there weren't sides to take, which was easy to see from where he was at college but harder to see back home where everything was smaller and more compressed. He could walk home from the library at night through the square, and everything would be very big and very small under the stars, and he didn't think anybody had a place like that back home.

And walking home like that, he imagined himself going home and saying as soon as he walked through the door, "Everybody's right. Everybody's right because it's crazy for Elham to be spending her time in that room, and it's perfectly reasonable for her to be spending her time there." And in his happiness at saying the truth of it, they would all have to consider that maybe there was something to it.

But it wasn't anything like that when he did go home, and the feeling had left him as he was driving back through the town, noticing how dark it was, wondering what all the people were doing in their houses. He couldn't bring with him the notion that everybody was right because there was nothing there to hold it but himself, and that wasn't enough in a place where the lines were already drawn.

So he stayed up late after his mother and father had gone to sleep and asked Elham about it in her room.

"What is all this about the drug counselor's office, Elham?" he asked. He thought that in fairness he ought to lean a little more to the side of crazy than to the side of perfectly reasonable, because he already knew she had a good answer.

"I like it there. Everybody's nice."

Oh Lord, he thought. He had to keep a straight face. His only chance of doing any explaining was in listening impartially to everyone. But some time when he was back at college he'd have to remember this conversation and laugh and laugh. She was off to a good start all right.

"What do they do there?"

"They believe each other, that's the main thing. If you tell them you're having a good day, they believe you, and if you tell them you're having a terrible day, they believe you. That's one of Ms. Devers's rules about the room: no judgment."

You mean to say, Massoud thought, that there is a place in high school where the people are trying not to judge each other? I would have taken drugs if I had known that.

"Maman said she talked with Ms. Devers."

"Yes. I don't know if it helped."

"That's a tough one to explain."

"I know."

"What about all your old friends?"

"I am still friends with Annie and Kelly. But Lauren and Caroline have changed. Maybe *they* think *I've* changed, I don't know."

"How?"

"They talk about people a lot. They put them into groups. Neither one of them does it as much individually, but when they're together, they do it a lot."

"What about Annie and Kelly?"

"They both smoke pot."

"They do?" Massoud was sure that his face showed that he still thought of them as little kids running around and riding bikes. Elham didn't say anything about it, though.

"Yes."

"Do they go to Ms. Devers's room?"

"No. They probably will next year. I hope they do. I've tried to tell them."

It was really funny, when he thought about it, that everybody was worried about Elham when here she was worried about the other kids in her class.

"Still," she said, "I'd rather spend time with people who are high all the time than with people who are talking about other people."

Massoud laughed. "Me too. The funny thing is that sometimes it feels like those are your only options in college too."

Elham smiled. "Well, I guess it's good that I'm getting some practice with it then."

She was really going to do some things in college, Massoud thought. If she kept going at this rate, she was going to come in knowing a lot of what he was just finding out.

They talked about other things for a while—books she was reading and teachers she had now whom he remembered and some stories about the little boy she babysat—until it came back around to where they knew it would, the arguments with her mother and father about her spending time in that room.

"I'll try to talk with them," Massoud said. "But it has to not look like I'm taking your side. If it looks like that, it'll push them over the edge. It'll push Maman over the edge for sure. She'll feel like here she is in this country where she doesn't understand either of her kids anymore. They already wish I was studying medicine instead of reading old Fyodor Dostoyevsky. So I'm already on shaky ground. So I'll have to listen to her tell me all of her side of it. I'll have to wait till she brings it up, and then I'll listen to her side of it. You have to remember that this doesn't make sense to them. 'Why would anybody hang out in the recovery room if they aren't in recovery themselves?' That's how it looks to them. I don't know. I don't know how you can explain it. It makes sense to *me*, but I grew up here and went to the same school, and I know how a room where nobody is judging each other can sound very nice. But I don't know how to explain it to them other than to listen to them all the way through first so that at least they know it's true that half of it's crazy. It's the other half that's the tricky part."

"I just wish they could trust me about it," Elham said. "I just wish they could trust me that it's the best place in the whole school."

"Elham," Massoud said, "think about how far the room by Ms. Devers's office is from anything they know."

"It's not, though, that's the thing. Not really. It's just a place where people see each other how they really are and accept it. I know they haven't had a place like that for a long time, but they can remember. They must remember from back home."

"I'd like to think they must remember from back home," Massoud said. "But I don't know."

They were quiet for a while.

"Well," Massoud said, "let me talk to them without any sides to it."

"Thanks, Massoud."

He hadn't thought of it as something to be thanked for. It was good for *somebody* to have a place like that that was honest and decent. It was *really* good if that somebody happened to be his sister. He wanted to see what would come of the whole thing. She was so much already that he was very excited to see everything she would become.

PEOPLE IN PROFILE

People in Profile was Mrs. Leavenworth's own creation. It had originally started with historical figures in general, but by the second year she had changed it to humanitarians. There ought to be a *good* reason children should get dressed up as people from history and sit on a stage being interviewed about their life and their historical significance as their parents watched. She didn't want them to think of it as Halloween. She wanted the night to take a side.

At six thirty, Cesar Chavez was being chased by Albert Einstein through the school hallway in their excitement for the show. They forgot that they had fought earlier that day in the playground. Mrs. Leavenworth had been upset to see it, but it had been a humanitarian fight. They both wanted a lot from the world, the way that a ten-year-old boy ought to want a lot from the world. Sometimes that got them in the way of each other. For just a moment she was glad to see them playing together again, before telling them to get backstage for the costume check.

Roberto Clemente looked at himself in a mirror. He was very excited to tell everyone that he was more than a baseball player. He was most excited to tell people that he died in a plane crash transporting supplies to earthquake victims in Nicaragua. He thought that if Helen Keller's older sister happened to be in the audience, she would be moved to hear it, and she would remember how moved she was the next time she saw him in the hall by the sixth-grade lockers. He took some practice swings, squinting in the Pittsburgh summer-day sun.

The first year after Mrs. Leavenworth had changed it, there was an appearance by Huey P. Newton. She hadn't known much about him. She hadn't known about the free-breakfast program for kids, and she hadn't known about the schools the Black Panthers had started where children learned yoga to manage their misbehavior. She had been very glad to learn it. The night had taken a side all right. She had felt glad to have left Maysburg and come to the city. Everyone she had left behind had felt balanced out by Huey P. Newton. And she had felt proud because she had known when she left that they would.

She wished now that everyone back home could see them, that they could see the caliber of people she spent her days among. She wished they could see Audrey Hepburn helping Charlie Chaplin put on his moustache. They wouldn't think there was any side to it then, because what could possibly be the side against that? Unless a part of them believed that it wasn't a person's job to be great. That was the thing she had feared about the place, and she had wanted to leave before seeing it become the thing she hated. She never really knew for sure, but in her truest heart she could see it, she could see them asking: Why tell children that they belong on the world stage?

It was good to know that the reason was clear when she saw them. It was in their faces. Maybe what they were saying back home was, why tell them that the world stage is the place for a man or a woman to be good? It's more important that they know how to do that on a smaller scale. All the little things her mother did for her father and all the little things her father did for her mother.

But she felt that if she could show them, they would know it didn't have to be one or the other. The larger scale could help with the smaller scale and the smaller scale could help with the larger scale. That was what she had learned in the city. Coming to San Francisco had helped her understand her town. They were trying there. That was the main thing.

In the corner of the stage, Mahatma Gandhi looked out from behind the curtain and saw his mother and father in the crowd. They were sitting one row and three seats apart. It was the first time he had seen them together in a long time. When he was younger, he would be happy whenever they were together, however much they would criticize each other and argue with one another. Now he didn't feel particularly happy or sad to see them together. He had figured out who he was with his mother, and he had figured out who he was with his father. They were not the same person.

Mrs. Leavenworth saw him looking out at the crowd, and she guessed what it was.

"How are you feeling?" she said.

"Okay."

"You saw that both your mother and father came?"

"Yes."

"I'm sure they're both very proud of you."

"Thanks."

"Do you remember that word you were working on?"

"Satyagraha. It means 'truth-force' or 'soul-force.'"

"That's right."

"I like truth-force better."

Mrs. Leavenworth smiled. He had taken in the presence of his mother and father together with a truth-force. At that moment she had no doubt that the smaller scale and the larger scale were very close together. And what could she possibly do about Mahatma Gandhi, she thought, that would be better than bringing him back? The whole point of the night was to show the children that none of the men and women were far away. She thought back to people from home who thought that *everything* was far away, too far away for them to deserve to know about. They had even thought San Francisco was too far away when she had first told them. All she could do now was be glad she hadn't believed them.

Five minutes before the program started, Mrs. Leavenworth saw Mahatma Gandhi's father stand up and walk to the other side of the room. Even one row and three seats had been too close. She hoped that Gandhi wouldn't see it, but she knew he would. The children all looked for their parents. They looked for them to say, here I am, and here's who I've been all along, quite possibly. She thought she should tell Gandhi so that he wouldn't come out and think that his father had left. When she did, he looked at her and said, "Okay." She thought that there was truth-force and soul-force in the way he said it.

When it was Gandhi's turn, he was accompanied to the front of the stage by John Lennon, where they sat in two chairs facing the audience. Mrs. Leavenworth thought that Gandhi looked glad to read the interview questions of John Lennon, as a way to not focus on his father moving across the room.

Then they switched, and John Lennon asked the questions. He asked about Gandhi's upbringing, his leaving for England and South Africa, and his becoming a lawyer. He asked about Gandhi's time in prison and about the Salt March. Gandhi demonstrated how he'd picked up a lump of salt at the sea at the end of the journey.

"I understand that you were also killed by an assassin's bullet, like me," John Lennon said.

"Yes," Gandhi said. "I was killed by a Hindu nationalist. England would not let India become independent unless it was split into India and Pakistan. I was opposed to the partition. I thought that Hindus and Muslims could live together peacefully. But some Hindus were angry because they thought I was being too generous to Muslims."

As he said it, Mrs. Leavenworth told herself not to look at his mother and father. There was a fire in her face just then, and it was not directed toward his parents' unpeaceful partition, although that was a part of it. It came from the way that the children fit right into the world's greatest humanitarians without much difficulty. For as long as she had been doing it, they always fell right into place. They weren't surprised to find themselves leading the Salt March. Their only surprise was that the Salt March was finally getting the attention it deserved.

"What do you consider to be your legacy?" John Lennon said.

"I consider my legacy to be the principle of satyagraha, which means 'truth-force' or 'soul-force.' I used this to show that aggression and violence were not the strongest weapons in the end. The strongest weapon was the one that could make a friend out of an enemy. That is what I meant when I said, 'An eye for an eye makes the whole world blind.'"

"Thank you. It's been a pleasure talking with you this evening, Mahatma Gandhi," John Lennon said.

"You as well."

The two boys smiled as they went to their spots at the back of the stage. There was something awfully nice about seeing the two of them together. Even though Mrs. Leavenworth had watched them rehearse a dozen times, she felt very glad they'd had a chance to meet.

After the program ended, Roberto Clemente looked for Helen Keller's older sister to see if she had been visibly moved by his death. She was talking on the phone but from the way he felt, he felt pretty sure that she had been.

Outside in the night, Gandhi's father hugged him as his mother stood waiting for him off to the side.

"You were wonderful," his father said.

Mrs. Leavenworth looked at him and thought that he looked like he knew he had been wonderful, in a way that he could hold inside him and did not have to let it out. The world stage was wherever they were, she felt. Just then she had a very difficult time believing that there could be any more of a world stage than the sidewalk outside the school at night.

Gandhi and his mother went to go home in one direction and Gandhi's father went in the other. It would be terrible to be Gandhi's father and to go home without Gandhi, Mrs. Leavenworth thought. Just having seen him at night would be enough to confirm your presence on the world stage, but it would certainly be nice to confirm that all the way through.

Three weeks later, Mrs. Leavenworth received a note from Heather, the recess teacher—"Just wanted you to know that the disputes in the sand yard among the boys in your class have stopped happening. Even the arguments on the basketball court have stopped. I heard one of them saying the other day when there was a question of a foul that they should handle it with truth-force. Not sure what this is, but if the whole school could do it, it would make my job much easier."

Mrs. Leavenworth took the note and put it in the boy's file, among the book reports and spelling tests. She thought for a moment of taking the file with her the next time she went home to visit, but she figured she ought to carry enough truth-force without it.

THE COUPLE

Among the homeless people of my neighborhood were a man and a woman who were very much in love. I would see them along Geary Street, pushing their belongings in a cart, and the woman would look very happy, and the man would look at peace. They looked like anybody else. They had their daily affairs to attend to, and they liked attending to them together.

They were not a part of the main groups of homeless people I would see. They were not part of the group that was often around the liquor store on Twelfth Avenue and that sometimes slept in the park across the street from my house. They were not part of the group that I would see lying on the grass in front of the library on sunny days. They were just their own pair, and they seemed to like it that way, and that seemed like it was enough.

One morning I saw the man standing at a bus stop. He was wearing clean clothes, and his hair was cut and his face shaven. I almost did not recognize him. But he did not look at peace like I had always seen him. He looked lost. He looked like he was trying to hold on to something steady in the middle of a great storm. He was waiting for the bus, and I figured that he had gotten some kind of job, but he did not look like he knew what the hell that meant. He looked like he knew that it was something that people did, but that that didn't help much.

I wondered if it had to do with the woman. The whole time that I had seen them, their homelessness was something that he wore outwardly more than she did. It was in his browned skin and clear, glassy eyes. It was a look that I had seen among the men carrying their packs on their shoulders in the Marina and Tenderloin Districts. It was a look that went with the sun, with the sun of San Francisco and the way that the moment was everything when you were in it.

I wondered if she had gotten tired of it and she had asked him to find a job as part of their beginning to get out of it. She always looked happy with him, but she also looked like a regular life with a home and a husband and things like that was not very far from her. She didn't look like it was something that she had forgotten about. I could see it in her clean, rosy face and her good, warm clothes.

If he was waiting at the bus stop like that for her, for their life together, I thought that was beautiful. He looked like a poet all the other times I had seen him; he looked like a poet toward every part of life except money, and now at the bus stop he looked like he was trying to go without that poetry for some money, and I knew that he really loved her.

I didn't see either the man or the woman for a while. And then one day I saw the man sitting in the park with the woman who used to ask for change in front of Cal-Mart. She was part of the Twelfth Avenue crowd. I used to see her in front of Cal-Mart back when I worked full-time at the school, and I would talk to her about her life. Once I had brought some of the kids down and had her talk to them about life, and she had always thanked me for that.

They were sitting in the park and drinking in the early afternoon.

"Hey, honey," she called out to me.

"Hello," I yelled.

"Going to the school?"

"Yes."

"That's great, that's great."

I could hear them laughing halfway down the block. They were having a good time. I had never seen him drinking before. With the woman with the rosy face, it seemed like they were always moving; it had seemed like their poverty wasn't something that kept them outside the world any. They would actually seem more inside the world than anybody, because the way they looked walking together went with things like dusk and spring better than anything else I saw among people. I couldn't think of anybody who had looked so much inside the same world that I was trying to be inside of, which was the world where you were taking notice of everything walking down the street, without trying to necessarily, just by having something inside you that let everything in. I had not seen anybody inside it like them, but I guessed I wouldn't be seeing it anymore.

It wasn't the worst thing in the world, I thought. She had wanted some kind of certainty in their life, and he had wanted some kind of freedom, and so they had gone their separate ways. The man did look happy sitting there on the grass in the sun. I thought of the last time I had seen the woman he was sitting with. She had seen me one night on Geary, and she had been telling me that it was a very good thing that I was working with kids, and then one of the homeless men who knew her had asked me why I was listening to the words of a heroin addict, and she had yelled at him, and it had been a mess.

Now she was sitting in a way that was womanly, and he was sitting like a man who had all kinds of time stretched out before him, and it looked like the beginning of a new romance. I hoped that they enjoyed it, and I thought that I probably shouldn't be sad about the end of the other relationship if the man didn't look sad himself. It was just that with the other woman, he didn't need a sunny day in the park, and I felt for certain that he didn't need alcohol. They had looked like the healthiest couple in the street to me, like they carried the best parts of the street with them and did their best with the difficult parts. The whole thing probably made some kind of statement about love and how much it was capable of and how much it was incapable of, but I decided to forget about it and wait until I learned the thing on my own if I was meant to learn it.

BOY IN PRISON

What an adventure, from waking up in the morning to going to bed at night, a life spent behind enemy lines, you might say, but if he said it, he would do so with such a smile as to disarm any enemy, as to leave such enemies intact but thinking, introducing them to their own country, already having accepted that they are the last to know, that they are the last to know about a prison cell in his country, about a prison cell in all the countries like his. It was all an adventure, because no place where he could find himself was any place he would've guessed as a boy in prison. I'm here on the ground with you, he could say to anybody, but I'm up in the sky too. On the ground, he could lose them, but from up in the sky, he could see them walking home, going to their own bed at night. They just didn't know, the ones he talked to in office buildings and parent-teacher conferences and neighborhood association meetings, and their ignorance was not the same as the torturer's lash, as the executioner's guns, but it was only because he had that view from the sky that he could see that.

It was an adventure because in the middle of driving to an appointment or calling a client, he could pick out anybody and he could speak to that person as though he were speaking from a prison cell. It was what they wanted to hear, wasn't it? Because they loved being part of the world, didn't they? And he wouldn't have said one word about himself and what he went through—he did not even talk about that with his children, who were of this country but of his heart—he just wanted to be able to speak from prison, because there were feelings there that could have shaped a world. What he would tell them would come from the heart of a prisoner, who had come out of prison with his body weakened and his heart absolute. It was a kind of speaking that he could not do without a smile, because he would be remembering men who had looked at death and greeted it like it was a child. They had lived there in prison in a way that they knew that death was inside of them. It became something to greet like a child because what they were really greeting was life.

And he was doing that living now in a country where that death was kept very far away. It was kept far enough away that he had learned quickly that they did not want to talk about it as though it bore any connection to them. That was fine—it just meant that he could not talk to them about life either. All that was left was floating, floating between the ground and the sky, and a man floated precariously when he first began floating, but it was a beautiful feeling once he began to gain some mastery over it. It was a very stable kind of floating because he knew better each day how right it had been to have been a boy in prison. If one country had so much and another country had so little, at least he had once been where he had had nothing, nothing except a kind of brotherhood that was unimaginable anywhere but prison. They had not had any doubt about succeeding, because they had already succeeded by being there.

And so anything he wanted to tell them now—the people around him—was not for himself but for them. He just had to float as he told it, because they were going to feel like they were losing everything if they really listened, and he had to float so that they would know that there could still be music and love after losing everything. And he had to float in their language, which was a very funny part of the whole adventure, considering that the only thing he had once known how to say was to tell them to go home.

He was in their home now, and he had to be a respectful guest, but it was awfully respectful of him to just float, to be ready to speak from a prison cell or not, and the truth was that at the end of the day as he lay in bed, he did not doubt that every word he had said came from there, in his own language or in theirs, every greeting and every parting, and it did not matter if a single listener knew that his words came from there. If they thought that that prison cell was not inside them, they were mistaken. If they thought that a prison cell many years ago in a country halfway around the world was not inside them, they were mistaken, and their mistakenness was nothing to dwell on, but it did bring enough humility to the night to let him think of the night as his own, at least his small part of it.

And that was a lot in a world that had kept right on building prisons and would keep on building them after he was gone from it. It was a lot to think of night with even a little of the sweetness of nights in prison, when men who would do anything for each other would be trying to do so until the last moment of wakefulness. The night had been so alive that it had felt no different from daytime. It was all work, and the darkest night was better than a sunny day if a man knew and loved his work. And he had learned since then to look at any work as that work. It was all the work he knew and loved just by being work, and doing his work with the same earnestness was the closest thing to a boy in prison, even if it was the work of buying and selling, a kind of work that he had dreamed in prison would be gone from the world by now, at least in the way that it left out poor people and poor countries. There was adventure in operating in that buying and selling with principles he had learned in prison, and nobody needed to know where those principles came from, because when he remembered them, it was not just him remembering them. It was men who had not had a chance to learn the adventures they would have past prison. They had been with him the whole time, so his adventures were theirs. His smile was theirs too, the way it could come out all by itself, because they would have been smiling at the whole thing too.

A wife and two children, he would have told them, and now I am in the country where our torturers were trained, where our king was paid. Can you imagine anything funnier? It was laughter because they would have known that his heart had not changed, that his struggle had not changed. And that laughter had not come out to them, but he had never stopped carrying it with him everywhere he went. There was nowhere he went that he was not talking to someone in a prison cell, after all. It was just a question of whether such people saw the walls around them. When two men who did spoke to each other, there was laughter in the most serious of their expressions. But most of the time, he had to provide the laughter. He had to provide it because the people were not used to being greeted as fellow prisoners. They were not used to thinking of prison as anything other than something so far away from them that the last thing they could do there was laugh. They were certainly not used to thinking of it as home.

And that was the craziest part of the whole adventure, that a boy in prison would be the one to grow up to tell them about home, to tell them about their home because of his intimacy with it, an intimacy he had not asked for but which he had found from seeking an intimacy with life. If there were going to be prison cells, then the only thing he had known for certain as a boy was that he was not going to make his life an effort to stay out of them. He would be thinking of the men in there either way at night in his bed; he had figured he might as well think about them with some intimacy. The important thing had been to take that dark night as a truth, because the darkest night became sunshine when two men faced it together. And after facing it had become who he was, he could take that sunshine with him anywhere and to anybody, and they did not always know where the sunshine they felt in themselves came from, but he could have told them if they asked; he could have told them going all the way back in memory, a man's memory and a country's, and if it led to a dark night inside them to hear it, he would still be there to tell them that there was something beautiful that followed.

THE RAIN CHECK

Sarah Warslow ran. She ran all over our town, and if it hadn't've been an island, she probably would've ran some more. I didn't fall in love with her when she was running; I did it when she was sitting still. But she sat still like somebody who knew herself. She knew that this afternoon she was going to run, either with the cross-country team or as practice for the cross-country season. It made as much sense to me as anything. What could you do with the town you grew up in besides dream of leaving it and know that you were going to miss it like hell? You could run through it, and somehow it would look like both.

We would see her on the way home from school, and I would join in with the other fellows, talking about her like part of the clockwork of our town. But it was more than clockwork, because she loved to run, but still it was a choice each time. I would see everything she *wasn't* doing as she ran. There was a world of pettiness and foolishness that she was simply setting aside, and I knew from the summer nights when I ran myself that it was hard to hate a place just after having run through it. She seemed like she knew that so well that it was a part of her all the time.

So I didn't know who better to fall in love with than someone who had the view of our town that she did. I wanted to take that world of pettiness and foolishness and simply set it aside too. I didn't want to indulge it, because Sarah Warslow was right: there were trees and mud puddles to run around and rain that fell on you and that you ignored, and there was solitude, and there was the way the afternoon looked bright when you ran even when the sky was gray. I wanted that to be all I saw when I looked at our town, and I didn't know what was so crazy about that.

A few times at school, I heard her talk about things that made her angry, and that was a great thrill. After all that, I thought, there is still room for anger too. My God. It was perfect. I considered anger my specialty the same way that she ran. Only anger was much less clear because I didn't know if I wanted to get good at it or not. That was another nice thing about watching her run. I thought of how good it must be to have a specialty that was yours, that you had chosen yourself instead of it being placed on you.

It seemed like it would be a good exchange. Only I didn't know if I would still have anger as a specialty if I was with her. I would have a new one, though: her. She could run, and I could think about her running. I could see every inch of our town in a new way. A beautiful girl who loves to run has been through here, and love would be enough to make the town beautiful even if she were always sitting still, but she is actively making it beautiful, by her presence, by answering the question of what a girl can do to belong to the town the way the trees and the rain and the gray sky belong to it. Which was a question that I thought everybody was asking but which sometimes seemed like it was just me. So I stayed quiet about all that when the other fellows talked about her like part of the clockwork. Even if she was like clockwork, they didn't see the beauty of that. You know what else is like clockwork? I wanted to tell them. Life. You think you're going to find a girl to exceed that?

The world at rest seemed like it was a pleasant diversion for her. School and its social concerns and its boys trying to be boys and its girls trying to be girls. It all seemed like an amusing break from when the world couldn't be moving. I didn't know how I was ever going to compete with a moving world for her, but I knew I had to show her that the world I carried in me had as much motion to it as our town when she ran. The good thing about that was that it did.

I just didn't get much chance to show that at school, where it seemed like the best way to keep the world inside me moving was to stay quiet. It seemed like whenever I was part of something loud and boisterous, a world was there all right, and it had something that certainly looked like motion; it just didn't seem like mine.

So I waited, hoping that she would see that the quiet in me was a real quiet and not an empty one, that it was like the quiet of our town when she ran. And when I got a chance, it was a beautiful thing because it happened in motion—it happened in the course of my motion—something that I had already been planning on doing anyway, which was to free the mice in the biology room who were going to be used in experiments.

I was sixteen years old and a reader of Dostoyevsky. I believed that what he had to say about freedom applied to humans and mice alike. They certainly hadn't done anything to deserve to be used in biology experiments. I imagined setting them free in the wet dark afternoon, and I felt their exhilaration at the touch of the air and the grass.

The biology room was empty at the time that I was in French class. That day, Sarah Warslow was sitting next to me. I told her what I was going to do. It was informational. I thought she had a right to know. If she happened to have gained an appreciation during her hours of running through our town for freedom, for nature, and for the very small creatures that populated it, that was a nice thing as well.

I told the teacher that I had to use the bathroom and left. I remembered how Sarah Warslow had smiled when I'd told her, but I tried to keep my focus on the mice. She had smiled like this was a little more than just the usual pleasantness of the stationary world.

The truth will come out, though, I thought, if you stay patient. A girl was a girl and mice were mice, and I hadn't thought they had anything to do with each other, but they had everything to do with each other. She looked like she didn't know that she had been thinking of the mice in the biology room, but when I told her, she seemed as worried about them as I was.

All right, I thought, I'm just going to have to be the one to tell people.

The biology room was empty. I went to the back room where the mice were kept. There was easy access to a window where I could have let them loose. But I couldn't do it. I started thinking about our biology teacher, Mr. Enloe. He was a nice man, and he told us stories.

Coming back to the classroom, I knew I must like Sarah Warslow very much because I was just going to tell her the truth. I had really thought I could do it, and then I couldn't. The only shame I felt was toward the mice. They had reason to be disappointed in me, but nobody else.

I was right about it. I told her what happened, and she didn't care about the decision. She saw the movement. She saw that I had a world in me that was far from stationary. She saw that I was reaching like that all the time. The mice in the cage just happened to be some fellows that I thought I could do something about. But I was worried about freedom and everybody's chance for it before them and I would be after them, and she saw that.

And I had a real chance back there. I had a real chance with a girl to do the thing that I saw Americans doing all the time, only it was real enough and true enough that it didn't feel like I was just trying to participate in an American thing, the way it had the year before when I had asked a girl to the high school dance. I had asked without knowing the first thing about what to wear or how to get there or any of that, and when she had turned me down, there was a small measure of relief in avoiding the corsages and cummerbunds and all the other American things that I wouldn't have to learn about just yet. But with Sarah Warslow, it all came from me, and even though she was American, it didn't feel like I was participating in an American thing when I called her up and asked if she would like to see a movie on the weekend; it felt like I was participating in myself. And when she told me that she couldn't do it because she was participating in a race out of town this weekend, she said the most beautiful American thing I had ever heard: she said she wanted a rain check.

She said it two times to make sure I understood. And I knew that a rain check, though it had a sad name, was a happy thing, a thing that a boy was supposed to be glad to give, and I was. Still, there was something that a boy who had given a rain check was supposed to do, and that was when I felt all the old things coming up in me again, all the old uncertainties that I felt sure I would know what to do with if only I were American, even a little thing like being able to go home and casually toss out the words "rain check" and have somebody know what I mean. And I felt angry at myself for having a little thing like that mean so much, because I knew what a rain check was, and that ought to be enough, especially since it *was* a happy thing; even if I hadn't known what it was, I could've told from the way she said it that it was a happy thing, and I felt angry at myself that I couldn't take the time to explain to my family what a rain check was, because they would be happy for me too, and it all seemed like it was going to be a long while before I figured out how to go from anger as my specialty to a specialty of her. The whole thing was too much for me because during the time of the rain check, I had to admit that I felt free of anger just seeing her run through town, so I didn't know who I would even be if I could actually go to a movie with her on the weekend, I didn't know that level of happiness was possible in America, because who would I be angry at then? When I looked around and thought, Nobody, it was a frightening thing.

I felt like the same guy who hadn't been able to let the mice free from their cage. I had gone a long time thinking that anger was freedom for an Iranian boy in America. In some ways, it was. But all the ways that it wasn't were how I messed up a perfectly good rain check in America, and I would still see her running through town after that, and I could add lost love to my list of specialties, which was closer. It was still pretty far away, but it was closer.

THE EASEL

One day in winter Amaury Prado was walking home from the library in the San Francisco Mission District when he saw an easel that somebody had thrown out with some other junk on the sidewalk. It was standing on its three legs as though it was just waiting for an artist. Amaury was twelve years old, and he had never thought of himself as an artist. But he picked up the easel and walked home with it over his shoulder, believing that he was on his way to a great career.

Amaury brought it home and put it in the garage. He could not wait until he could take it out and set it up and paint different places in his neighborhood. It was a cold and gray winter, and he figured he would wait until spring. He would set it up in front of his house, and he would paint the people and houses on his street. He thought of how happy and proud the people would be when they saw him painting them. They would say hello to him, just enough so as not to interrupt him. A boy with an easel, he thought. What else could he possibly need?

The easel looked much better standing in the garage than folded up against the wall. It looked like the world wanted him to be an artist. He would look at it each morning and look forward to the spring. The easel was waiting with him, nobly and patiently. That's how I ought to wait for things, Amaury thought. The easel was already beautiful, before there was any artwork sitting on it, before an artist even came along. It seemed to know what it could do, when the time came.

He thought of the easel sometimes when he was at school. A man did his real learning by himself, he thought. The learning he did at school was okay, but there was something he could learn at the easel that he couldn't learn anywhere else.

One day he came home, and his father, who drove the owl bus for the city at night, was not asleep as he usually was.

"I'm sorry, Amaury," he said. "When I came in this morning, I pulled in too close to your easel. I cracked one of its legs."

Amaury ran to the garage. The easel was leaning to one side, like a wounded animal. The break hadn't gone all the way through, but it was just barely hanging on.

Amaury got some medical tape and taped up the break. He rolled the tape around several times, until the leg was bulging.

How would it be now when he took the easel out to paint the people and the places? The people would laugh at his easel, and they would forget to be proud of themselves for having somebody paint them and their street. He didn't want to paint them laughing like that. Even if somebody saw the painting afterward and thought that it was just a friendly laughter. He wanted to paint them going about their day.

It rained for days and days in February, and it seemed like spring would never come. Amaury got used to seeing his easel with a taped-up leg. Still, sometimes he thought of how he should've kept it folded against the wall before. Then he wouldn't have minded all this rain, and his only thought would've been of when he could take the easel out. The whole street would've known when it was spring then. It must be spring, they'd say to each other, because the artists are out with their easels. And he'd be too busy to notice the people, same as the birds and the trees and everything else that came alive in spring.

When there was a break in the rain, it seemed hopeful again. The city looked so beautiful when the sun broke through for even just a little while that Amaury thought the people would care more that an artist was painting than about his easel having a bandaged leg. They would know where the priorities lay. But the rain would start up again, and he wouldn't be so sure.

It would be lousy if the accident kept him from a great career in art. Something didn't add up, though: his father was a nice man, and he had apologized. That was all he could do. Maybe it was an artist's job not to care if the people he was painting laughed at his easel. Maybe he was supposed to paint them the way he *wanted* them to be. If that was how it was, then it seemed like being an artist was much harder than he realized, and it was possibly the hardest thing in the world.

You couldn't start thinking of how you wanted them to be only when you stood at your easel. You had to be thinking of that before you got there, at least a little bit, at least enough to see a little crack of how they could be that would lead to the big picture. It might be a very small crack, but that was all you needed. Somehow a small glimpse of that was as big as a view from the top of the hills of the city where he'd seen artists standing with easels before.

And he felt foolish for having brought home the easel because real artists knew they were artists before they found an easel on the street. Even if he was right that an artist ought to paint people the way he wanted them to be, he knew he was not great at painting or drawing. He was just a guy who liked easels. That was not enough of a reason to keep one, though, and the next time the rain broke, he took the easel and left it in an empty lot on Valencia Street, leaning against a fence beside a wall that had a mural of the Aztecs and Tenochtitlán.

His father was going to work that evening, and when he passed by the lot, he saw the easel leaning against the fence. He recognized its taped-up leg. He didn't know what it meant. He liked the sight of the easel in the garage as well, and he still felt bad for having cracked its leg. He thought about it all night as he drove up and down Geary Street. It made him sad to think of the easel leaning against the wall like that, and it made him sad to think that Amaury had given up on it. When he drove past the lot in the morning, the easel was gone.

In the afternoon, when Amaury came home, his father was not asleep as he usually was.

"You got rid of the easel," his father said.

"Yes," Amaury said. "I'm not an artist, Pop. I'm just a guy who likes easels."

"What else do you like?"

"I like books."

His father was quiet. "If you like easels," his father said, "that's a perfectly good reason to keep an easel around."

Amaury saw that the easel mattered to his father. It wasn't just something he'd happened to bump into with his car.

"You're right, Pop."

"You don't have to be an artist to have an easel around."

"You're right."

Amaury went to his room to read his book, and he thought that even if he wasn't an artist, there sure was something he understood about art, which wasn't only that a guy who could paint ought to paint people the way he wanted them to be; it was that the moment of art was the moment when the way he wanted them to be turned out to be the way they were and then some, and he hoped that even if he didn't paint them, he would be able to do something with that someday.

THE WORLD IS MY HOME

Just before he approached the young man and young woman walking on the college campus in Dresden, Germany, in the late evening, Arvin Khiavchi thought, Even if we don't find a place to stay tonight, the world is my home. As long as there is a sun beginning to set, and a group of Arab students playing soccer on the grass, and a German man who gave us a ride today from Berlin, the world is my home.

The young woman, he figured later, must have agreed with his assessment, because when he asked the couple if they knew of any hostels in the area, she said, "You can stay with me."

How does a thing happen like that? Should I start drawing some conclusions about either myself or Germany or the world? he thought.

He went to tell his friend Allie Dagneau. He was on a pay phone calling hotels.

"Everywhere is full. Do they know of a place?"

"Yes."

"Where?"

"Her house."

They laughed and didn't understand it and proceeded to go on their best behavior. They didn't understand when she took them to her house and gave them two warm beds. They didn't understand that night when she and the young man took them to a restaurant inside a castle. They didn't understand the next morning when she woke up early to go to the bakery to bring them fresh bread for breakfast.

But Arvin's surprise was that she could see something in them that went with her taking them in and showing them the city. Not that there was nothing to see. He knew there was something because all that he and Allie were concerned with since they'd left Utrecht was everything. And he and Allie were concerned with everything before then, but when two good friends were concerned with everything in motion, that was it—it was the last word. There was no getting closer to living than that, and his only surprise was that she could see it so quickly and clearly, which he felt a little bad about because maybe he shouldn't have sold people so short.

"Would she have done this for any two guys?" Allie said that first night when they were in their beds.

"I don't know. It's too much to think about."

"What do you mean?"

"I mean it's obvious to us that we're two guys to take in. We rode in the back of a van driven by a goddamn traveling video-game salesman coming from Utrecht, and we almost slept in a field that night. We met my cousins in Hannover, and we listened to their dreams. And we didn't say a word from Berlin to Dresden because the man driving us didn't speak a word of English and we didn't want to exclude him. Can she see all that? I don't know. It beats the hell out of me."

Allie laughed.

"Is the world a beautiful place?" Arvin asked.

"It might be."

"I know I ought to be glad to hear you say that, but you know what it sounds like to hear you say it? It sounds like work."

"What kind of work?"

"The kind that is going to make who we are when we're traveling be who we are when we're just living in one place."

"You think it can be done?"

"I think it's the only choice."

The next day she took them to a museum, and by then it didn't seem strange anymore. They were three friends, and it would have almost seemed stranger if she *hadn't* taken them in. She talked with both of them together, and at different times she talked with each of them alone, and at those times they each fell a little in love with her, as a way of understanding her. A young man ought to fall a little in love with a young woman who would do that, they thought.

They clowned around a little bit for her, exaggerating their personalities, telling embarrassing stories of each other that seemed less embarrassing far away from where they'd happened. Her laughter was beautiful, because she looked like she was not overflowing with it as she might've once been. The whole thing was nice, because they knew if they stayed here, one of them would feel enough to want to know exactly what the story was with the young man she'd been with on the first day, but for a couple of days, it was okay.

Arvin and Allie didn't think anymore of whether she would do this for any two guys. It was enough to be in it. No matter who they had been and what they had been doing to make her invite them home without a second's thought, their only job was to keep being and doing it, and since they hadn't been *trying* to be anything other than who they were, the worst thing they could do was to start trying now.

In the afternoon they went by train to a spot she said would be a good place from which to catch their next ride. Allie fell asleep on the train. Arvin looked out the window and saw an area outside the city with rows of beautiful gardens and what looked like very small houses beside them. He built a whole vision of who he imagined lived there: they were all people who'd come to the conclusion that gardens were more important than houses. It was a fair enough conclusion, he thought, having already seen a few European cities and having seen the same lostness and vastness he'd seen in American cities. The townspeople had all decided that it was worth living in very tight quarters if it meant being able to step outside to the immediate presence of flowers and vegetables and fruit trees.

Arvin asked the young woman about it. She explained that they weren't houses. They were plots that people in the city rented to garden, and the little houses were their sheds. She told him that her dream was to one day have one of the plots, only there was a very long waiting list.

"That is what I like to do," she said, "something with my hands, something with the earth. I don't really like to do anything else. If I had my choice, I would read a little each day. I would go and see my grandmother. But mostly I would like to work with the earth, to make something, to produce something. I am studying psychology, but I don't know what I would like to do with that."

All these girls in America that I felt sad for, Arvin thought, and along the way I was assuming that my sadness was confined to America. I didn't know they were thinking the same things in Germany. I didn't know they were dreaming of days of reading and seeing their grandmothers and gardening.

Sometimes the world felt too big to be his home. If there were girls wondering and dreaming like that in Germany, then they were doing so everywhere. He couldn't sit and listen to all of them. Even when he sat and listened to one of them, the world was just barely his home. It was the infinite depth of one person, more than miles they had traveled or distances between cultures—that was the greatest obstacle to the world being his home. Yet somehow it was the greatest opportunity too.

Having Allie around was good, because some time later when they were standing on the side of the road again like they had gotten used to doing, he could tell Allie about the young woman's dream, and then the two of them would carry it together, like a water bucket they were carrying between them, and even if his side would be a little heavier sometimes because Allie was distracted by something along the path and would end up carrying his side too low, Arvin was still happy to be carrying it with someone. It was an opportunity to see exactly what he carried, in step with the day when he could carry it by himself.

They came to a spot by the train station where they said good-bye. They thanked her for everything, and they wondered if they would ever see her again.

After she left, Arvin told Allie about the poetic vision he'd had, of the people living in little houses beside their gardens.

"What do you do with a vision like that when you turn out to be wrong?" Arvin asked.

"It still counts," Allie said.

Arvin didn't tell him about the young woman's dream. They were very good friends, and it was enough to know that he could. And he was beginning to think that if the world was really going to be his home, he was going to have to get used to its mystery; he was going to have to get used to doing something like listening to a young German woman's dream and holding it somewhere where he didn't have to answer it, where he didn't have to collapse at the thought of all the dreams of the young women he didn't know, all the dreams of the young women who were now old women, and the men too, both young and old. He was already good with everything he saw, even seeing visions that weren't there, but he was going to have to get just as good with everything he didn't know and couldn't see and would never be able to touch and would certainly never be able to tell somebody about and would most certainly never be able to always have a good friend like Allie around to tell either. He was going to have to get good at something infinite, but the infinity he had come across a few moments ago made him think that it was possible.

I might've been the only guy walking around through Jimmy's Old Car Show and Picnic looking at all the big 1950s cars and thinking, I guess this is why they overthrew Mossadegh back in 1953 and brought back the Shah. It was funny because I looked at the American people and I knew that a lot of the ones who were alive back then didn't know about it and a lot of the ones who weren't alive didn't know about it either, but there was nothing to do but look at their cars and look at their pride standing next to the shine of the chrome and want to tell them that if this was just a by-itself thing, if it didn't go back to Iran and 1953 and to a lot of other places and times, I would be all for it, but it did go back to those places and times, so I could only be all for some part of it, which had more to do with seeing them than with seeing their cars. A person has more of a chance of looking like more than you see before you than a car.

I saw Jimmy drive by on his Park and Rec mower and called out to him.

"Shh," he said. "This car show's been around for eighteen years and most people still don't know if there's a real Jimmy or not. That's the way I like it. Are you having fun?"

"Sure. I like looking at all the different people."

"The people? The cars are the stars. That's been my motto from the beginning. That's why I don't want anyone to know if there's a real Jimmy. Next thing you know, they'll be wanting to take their picture with me. Who needs it? The cars are the stars."

"Okay, Fred."

"That's it."

It's a blues thing to be alive, and it's a blues thing to be alive in America and to be from a country that you would've stayed in if it hadn't been for what America had done to it. And it's the funniest thing in the world to set out to tell Americans about that. I mean funny as in if you do set out to do that, you had better keep a laugh with you at all times.

Some men and women were leaning against cars from the fifties, and they were dressed in the style of the fifties. "What is it about the fifties?" I asked.

"It was before Vietnam," said Jimmy, who'd been there.

I guessed he was right, but it was during a lot of things and after a lot of things too. Still, if you were going to be in America, you couldn't let Americans see that you carried 1953 around with you all the time as an Iranian, just like you couldn't let them see that you carried 1954 around with you all the time as a Guatemalan. You had to wait until it came up, and then you had to act like you suddenly just remembered. It's a funny thing.

But something comes out when you keep all that stuff in. The grass and the trees and the smell of Golden Gate Park, where Jimmy had been a gardener since he'd gotten back from the war. The park through time, and San Francisco in 1953, which was a place that I didn't have any hatred for. I even felt happy for San Francisco in 1953 and the people dressed the way they were and riding around in those big cars the way they did. I guessed that if I had been around then, I wouldn't have known about Mossadegh either. And then all kinds of years went by, and whenever somebody mentioned 1953—I suppose everybody wanted to remember their 1953—I'd be back to the same place I always ended up when I thought about these things, which is that if I do intend to tell Americans about our 1953, I have to hold all the 1953s—including the one where the Anglo-Iranian Oil Company refused to allow a democratic Iran to have some say in its own oil production and the one where American kids were driving through Golden Gate Park with a general feeling that life was okay. And I was prepared to do it—I had been doing it long enough that I knew they could be done together—but I just wished somebody would realize how tiring it is.

"I don't go in for the dressing-up myself," Jimmy said. "It's not the fifties any more. But some people like it."

"It's hard to be in the time you're in," I said. "Maybe they're just taking a break."

He looked at me like this was as philosophical as he wanted to get. I understood.

I knew that the cars were the stars, but I couldn't understand how anybody could come to an old car show and not think that the most interesting thing was the people. Look at them, I thought. Look at them wanting their time alive to mean something like it did in 1953 or any other time, and look at them succeeding at that just by wanting it. I don't know who ever succeeded at living just by wanting to like human beings do, and I knew a part of me was always going to ask, What kind of living is it when they are remembering a 1953 that doesn't care about my 1953, about the 1953 that my heart is made of? Well, it was living—there was no getting around that. Hell, there was a little boy back then who'd loved cars, who'd grown up to start a car show in Golden Gate Park where he didn't want anybody to know who he was. That was enough to make it living all by itself. And it was no kind of fun to start thinking about one place being anymore living than another. The most living place was wherever a person happened to be. And I couldn't start thinking that 1953 was any more living than today, because the principles that had made it a year in my heart were still around, in whatever form they happened to be. The American people dressed like 1953 believed in those principles too, if somebody could explain those ideas to them in the right way, and I knew that my life in America was going to be made of believing in their 1953 and in treating them like they could believe in mine, and it was just going to be a question of which one when.

It was theirs today, and all that meant was that mine had to be inside me, which is where it was used to being anyway. Maybe that was the only place they could be together for now, but I didn't believe that was how it was *always* going to be. It was just a Sunday afternoon in Golden Gate Park, but I looked at the American people, and I believed in a time when everybody's 1953 could be there together, and the cars might still be the stars, but I didn't think so. They were beautiful, and I could see how a man could *make* them the stars, at the expense of everybody even knowing who he was, but sometime in the world I would like to go to a place where the people were the stars. They had enough in them to do it. They had years and worlds inside them. If the people were the stars, they could let in years they didn't know about, and it would only add to them, not take anything away. It would be adding sadness and lostness, but it would still be adding. They'd know that adding those things is part of what made them stars. It wouldn't be the only thing that did it, but it would be half of it.

In the meantime I could still do it one person at a time. I could still do it tomorrow at the cafe with Jimmy, not as an agenda but as something that just happened to come up.

It was really only fair. I was letting their 1953 in in good faith, and it was true that I was in America and they were not in Iran, but the important thing about Golden Gate Park was its grass and trees, which were like the grass and trees in a park in Iran, where we all *could've* been, and there was no point in not being prepared for anything, it seemed to me.

"Every one of these cars is a memory," Jimmy said.

"I believe it."

"Did I ever tell you about how we used to race out there on the Great Highway," he asked, "back when I had a Mustang?"

"No," I said. "I'd like to hear about it, though."

YOU DON'T LEAVE

They figured he had a girl up in Bellingham, and Armon didn't know how to tell them that Caroline Cooper was a girl but that it wasn't that sort of thing. He had certainly hoped it would be that sort of thing for a long time, all through college, but in their third year she had told him about something that he couldn't tell them about. It was her father, and she had been a little girl. When she had told him, he had gone home and looked in the mirror and cried. He had asked her later if she had told many other people, and she had said she'd told a few of her friends but that he was the only man she had told. He had asked her why, and she'd laughed and said, "Men leave. You don't leave."

He'd left in the morning and drove the one-and-a-half-hour drive up the highway, and he thought, It's just one day. It was easier not to dream of her now that she was in another city, and seeing her would knock him back a ways, but he could get over it. Along the way he saw many beautiful things that he thought he would tell her about, and then he thought maybe he would and maybe he wouldn't.

She lived in a little house across the street from a park. The smell of the place sent him back to her old apartment and to nights they laughed together and a few nights she had cried. When he saw her, her whole face turned warm and open, like there was nothing she wouldn't trust him with. I wonder what her face looks like when she opens the door to the men who leave, he thought.

It was nice, though, being here. He told her about a few of the things he had seen along the way. She listened so effortlessly that he found himself hoping that those men have at least had some things to say.

They walked from her house through a trail that ran into town. It had been difficult for her to come to Bellingham for graduate school because it had been where her father had gone after he'd left. He'd had a store and gotten to know a lot of people. She said she had a fear that she would meet someone who knew him and thought he was a good man.

"It's crazy, I know," she said.

"It's not so crazy."

"Well, it's not as if we have the same last name anymore, so there's no reason that someone would make that connection. Unless they thought I looked like him, but I don't think I look like him."

"It's not crazy because what he did was crazy."

She smiled. "Yes," she said.

They walked past a reservoir where they could look out and see an old cannery.

"It's funny," Armon said. "You look at an old factory, and if it was still in use, I might not think about it very much. But as soon as it's abandoned, I wonder about it a lot."

"I think you would still like it if it was in use."

"You're right, but I would think about it differently."

"How?"

"I don't know. It's easy to like old, abandoned things."

"They have stories."

"Right. Things in use have stories, but it's harder to see them."

This was probably something that the men who left didn't do. They didn't go around making declarations about factories in use and abandoned ones. They probably knew how to talk in a way that moved naturally to whispering in her ear and putting their arm around her in the grass. Talking of factories wasn't the thing.

They walked through the park where the trail ended.

"It's nice to see you," she said.

"Nice to be seen." It was a joke he didn't mean, just an effort to keep his heart up. She smiled at the joke and the effort both.

"I appreciate you driving all the way up."

"I like driving," he said. "And of course it's nice to see you too," he added. He didn't need to say it. The benefit of the doubt was something he had already won, and he was sad to realize it. Steady and dependable. But what did he have to show for it? No girl in Bellingham and no girl back in Seattle either.

If you wanted to, if you were into that sort of thing, you could walk into any of the bars in his neighborhood and join a table where a group of young men were sitting together and fall into a conversation about how girls did not like young men who were nice. Even if they were right, he was still glad that he had met Caroline Cooper. He was still glad that he had known her the way he had and that he had seen the part of her that she had shown him. She had opened up a world to him. It was a place of feeling. A person could hold their love and hold their hate, and if they were sure of them, they could let them come out the way they would, and they didn't have to rush them. He felt like he had all the time in the world with her because a day was so full.

And then there was the way she listened. She made herself comfortable when he spoke. She could be walking alongside him, and she would still give him the feeling that she was leaning back in an easy chair when he began to tell her his feelings about canneries. That was what made a woman to him. And yet there was something in her womanliness that he couldn't meet.

Once he found that thing . . . , he thought. But it seemed like it was too late with her.

The one thing he wouldn't do, the one thing he felt proud to have not done so far, he wouldn't ask her: What did those men do? What did they do before they left?

And the truth was, he didn't want to know. If what they did meant that she laughed at the thought of telling them about her father, he didn't want to know.

He almost felt like he had skipped girls and gone straight to women, only he didn't know what to do once he got there. In college there was a kind of girl that he told himself he ought to forget about Caroline Cooper with and go after instead. A denim skirt and low-cut sneakers. Maybe she had books that she lived and died over and maybe she didn't. And one or two times he had found her. But he would look for the tragedy, either personal or philosophical or both, and if it wasn't there, he felt like the girl was only telling half the story.

"Let's go up to the square," she said. "There are some murals there I think you'd like to see."

He laughed to himself inwardly—he still hung on her words, hoping for a slight change in the phrasing: *There are some murals I want to show you.* He would drive up *every* Saturday for a sentence like that.

They walked up to the square, and he thought of how much he would have to say about the people of the town if they were going to end the night together. He would love them, first of all, and they would know it by looking at him. He would let them all in, and it wouldn't matter that it was his first time walking through their town.

She was right. The murals were beautiful. One of a whale gave him a peaceful feeling. It was nice to think of something that big swimming thoughtfully under the water's surface. There was more to the world than what he could see.

"I like the whale the best," she said.

"It's nice," he said.

"I'm glad that I live close to the water at least," she said. "I don't think I could live somewhere where I couldn't look at the ocean."

"Yes," he said. "I like the ocean the way it is here."

"How do you mean?"

"It doesn't have to make a big deal about itself. It just shows up on your way to town."

She laughed.

"The whole town is like that," she said. "It makes it a good place to study, I suppose. Not as much to do as in Seattle. You must be having fun there, though."

He shrugged. "There are a few places I go to." He did not want to show her that her absence was often the main feature of those places, especially as it got nearer to the end of the night. Somewhere between the truth and her trust in him, that was where he was aiming. But he knew too how perceptive she was.

"Let's look for a place to have lunch," he said.

They went to a place that had fish sandwiches and sat outside and watched the people go by. They sat together, and maybe some of the people going by thought they were a young man and a young woman together, and maybe some of them didn't, but either way it didn't matter too much.

The thing that he respected about Caroline Cooper was that she had given him a chance in college—not to be one of those men but to walk away after she'd told him she did not feel the same way. It was only after he'd stuck around that she'd told him.

They walked around town after lunch and stopped in a few shops. They talked things over with some kids running a lemonade stand back in her neighborhood.

They sat on the steps outside back at her house, drinking coffee. Maybe it's for the best, he thought. It would be too fine. It would be too fine to have the day go by as easily as this and have the night go by so easily too. Where would be the tragedy in that?

They watched the kids playing in the park across the street. It wasn't the first time he had watched kids playing with her and thought about her as a little girl. He knew a little bit about how to do it. She didn't want him to ignore it, and she didn't want him to fall apart over it. She just wanted him to know it and to hold that knowledge.

But even so he felt a thought coming up in him. She was beautiful, and the dusk was falling, and it would be a very wonderful thing to stay, and he felt the thought coming up: If you hadn't told me about your father, I would've left too. Not as quickly as those other men and not under the same circumstances, but I would've left. I'm a man too.

Something wouldn't let him say it. Suppose he did—what would the world look like on his way home? Nothing. It would look like nothing. As long as he held it inside him, the world had a chance.

"I like it here," she said. "I feel like I am getting stronger, like I am getting healthier."

"That's great," he said.

If he hadn't been lost in his own thoughts, Armon might have heard that inside her words she was saying that she was beginning to see a time when the man who stayed the night and the man she told her heart to would be the same man. But he didn't, and a little while after that, he stood up and embraced her and told her that it had been very good to see her, which it had been, and he began to set out for home, and for about the first third of the drive he went back and forth between wondering if he was the saddest man on the road or the most foolish, until he couldn't do that anymore, and he decided for about the next third that he was actually the one most in awe of the setting sun, until an unspeakable happiness came over him in the last third, driving in the darkness, something that carried him all the way to the bar around the corner without going home, where the fellows were sitting just where he thought they would be, where they saw him come in with an aliveness that made them not even know how to ask him about it, too amazed that he had made it all the way up to Bellingham to see a girl and still made it back in time to have a beer with them.

TAKE OUR DAUGHTERS TO WORK DAY

Take your daughter with you to the place where you work, the school had said. Take her to see where you work so that she can see herself working someday. Girls need to see that they can become anything they want to be.

I do not want her to see where I work, Nasrin thought. I do not want her to see me sweeping up hair after a customer leaves. I would rather tell her about Iran, about the school and my classroom and how the other teachers used to come to me for advice. I would rather tell her about that.

But the girl cried and said that all the other girls were going to go, that she would be the only girl at school that day if she didn't go, and her husband said that he would take her to the restaurant, but he was the night manager after all, and the girl said she didn't want to go to the restaurant, she wanted to go to the hair salon, and Nasrin cursed the school because up until then she had felt glad and proud to be working there, but all that fell when she thought of her daughter seeing her there, and she thought of going down to the school and telling the teacher that she would have to take her daughter to Iran to do this right.

Let me explain, she would say. I was a teacher there. When I wanted the girls in my class to know that they could be anything they wanted to be, I would show them myself. I did not ask their mothers and fathers to do it because I did not know their mothers and fathers. I knew myself. That is what a teacher is supposed to know. She is supposed to know herself so that she has something to teach. There is math and reading and writing and history, but along the way of all of that, a teacher is supposed to know herself.

Now I am here in America, she thought. Okay. I am not a teacher. I am a hairdresser. Okay. I can do it. I can take who I am with me every day and find a place for myself there. But not with my daughter watching. Not if she sees me there without having ever seen me in Iran.

Maman, the girl said, it doesn't matter what you do. I am proud of you either way.

And Nasrin cried and thought: it was a way children were taught to speak in America, to tell their mothers that they were proud of them either way. And she thought of how her daughter would never see her where she had been most herself, where she could move with so much certainty, where she knew the ins and outs of everything—the city itself and the school and relationships and family life. She would never see her walk with the city as her background as though it was hers alone, having earned it, having earned it from another day of aiming to be exactly who she wanted to be.

She cried, and the girl cried, and Nasrin's husband stood in the room and felt in some distant part of his mind how it was the same crying. It was the same crying but he couldn't say that because nobody wanted to be told that her crying was anything other than her own crying. This crying isn't starting now, he wanted to tell them. It started ten years ago, when we left Iran. It is nobody's fault. It is not even the school's fault for asking. He left the room and went outside. His neighbor was collecting the mail.

It is the same crying, Nasrin's husband said.

What is? his neighbor asked.

My wife and my daughter are both crying about each other, but it is the same crying.

Ah.

Yes. He went back inside. They had stopped crying and gone to their rooms.

I'll take her with me to the restaurant, her husband said. I'll go in the morning and make the food orders.

He went to tell his daughter.

In the girl's room, the daughter asked, Baba, why does she tell us so much about the place at night when she comes home? Why does she have so many stories about the people there? I thought she would be glad that I could finally come and see everybody there.

From the next room Nasrin heard her daughter and thought: It is not the same. It is not the same when I tell it and when you see it. When I tell it, I am myself again. I am standing in front of a classroom again. It is the closest I can come to standing in front of a classroom. I can speak in Farsi, and I can know that everybody understands. But if that is the issue, then I won't talk about it. If I have to let you see it to tell it, I won't tell it.

For the next few days Nasrin did not say anything about her day at the salon when she came home in the evening. But after a week she began to feel the way she felt in the middle of the summer in Iran, when she would miss the school and the classroom and the kids very much. And she started back again slowly, telling one funny story about a customer that day. Her husband and her daughter listened eagerly. And pretty soon she got rolling again, talking of her coworkers and Americans and all their ways, and her daughter listened and figured that even if her mother would not take her to work, at least she was taking her somewhere.

THE THEATER OF WAR

Fields of battle throughout history where men had fought and died had culminated in the beautiful sand dunes of the Presidio of San Francisco serving as the theater of war for a group of students from Presidio Hill School, and the young man who had brought them there thought that that must have often been the case—that even the sight of the bay in the distance added to the spirit of battle for its participants rather than contrasted with it. Each group had probably believed that nature was on its side, and nature hadn't been able to tell anyone that it wasn't on either side, or at the least that it was on both sides, or that most of all it was on the side of those who had laid down their arms or had never picked them up in the first place. They were the ones most in need of something on their side anyway.

Something could be said about the dead and nature too, if the young man were to go in that direction. They were so much on the side of nature that they joined it. It did not feel like there was any contrast in being among the children and thinking of the dead. It did not feel like there was any contrast even in a place so alive with the warm sun and the cool of the eucalyptus trees. And anyway, in the time that he was alive, war was a thing that very much included children.

There were some facts to consider: When he was a boy, a shelter of branches would have looked very much like a fort to him too. A stick would have looked like a gun. And running and hiding behind a tree to spy on the enemy would have seemed like the best thing to do about the existence of trees and the spaces between them.

There was a thrill in the order of a chain of command, soldiers reporting to colonels and colonels reporting to generals. And there was the love expressed at the moment of death, for one's side by the dying, before being miraculously saved, and for one's dying comrade by swearing revenge.

He knew all that to be true, and he didn't know where else they were supposed to get all that from, but at the same time, he wanted them to know about the children in the world who could not afford to play games about war. Those kids were a part of him as much as the kids in front of him were a part of him. And because the ones in front of him were kids, they were less likely to think that something was being taken from them when they learned about somewhere else. It was a park, and the idea was that what kids ran off to do in a park was natural, as natural as the bay and the sun and the trees, but what was the difference between children and men when it came to nature? All the adventure in their game was true, but something else was true too, which was that the men fighting wars had played them as children, and nobody had tried to tell them that peace was as much of an adventure. Just to be a voice in the wilderness, and he might not be able to tell them, but he might be able to show them.

"General, they've captured one of our men!"

The general thought for a moment. "It could be a trap," he said. "Two men are going to have to stay and guard the fort. They could be after our weapons." He motioned toward the pile of sticks beside the tree stump that served as a lookout point.

When only the guards were left, they were approached by a tall man who was a stranger in the kingdom.

"I bring a message from the other side," he said.

"What is it?"

"They say that they don't know what the point of all this fighting is. They say that they would like to meet halfway between the two forts and have a tea party."

The guards were suspicious. "We don't believe you. Why have they captured one of our men?"

"They did that because they were scared. They saw him in their territory, and they reacted. They don't want to keep him, though. They want peace, just like your people do."

"We don't want peace. We want war!"

As they spoke, two enemy fighters crawled up the hill behind the guards toward the weapons cache. They saw their teacher, smiled, and put a finger over their lips. The young man saw them and knew that they were going to get some of the sticks. But if they got too close, they might try for the bigger ones, and he didn't want any fighting over those because somebody might get hurt. He waited long enough to show respect for their stealthiness, and then he let his stare linger long enough to make the guards turn around and notice them. They made away with a few small sticks, and the guards felt proud to have thwarted a larger disaster.

Well, he thought, timing was something that didn't need a war for a man to feel like he had a good sense of it. It certainly was something that a man could have in peacetime.

Which was why it was more than a joke. Joking was the form it took, but it was all very practical: he wanted to give them two or three things they could do outside war. He didn't know if it was natural, but the *forms* of war at least that they were using had been given to them by men, and a man ought to balance it out.

It was funny how much children helped in trying to be a good man. When it was going well, it was a job in which he was clocking in to do his best at everything and never really clocking out at the end of the day, just changing scenes. Who he was to children stayed with him past the time with them and mixed with who he was to himself so that the two were very close.

He walked across the sand to the other side and checked on how the battle was progressing. Threats were being issued and demands being made for the captured soldier's release. This was why it was thought to be natural: The forms were given to them, but the actions and emotions seemed to come from themselves. They seemed to come from themselves as though they had been waiting for something to come from themselves like that.

Maybe they had been. But maybe he had been too. Maybe he had been waiting for something to come from himself all this time that he had been reading and learning about war and spending his days among children far away from it. All this time that he had been accepting the contrast, doing so by bringing some rules to it, like not reading news of war in the morning before seeing the children, waiting until afterward and reading it at night, when he would be filled up from a day with them in a way that made the reading easier, or at least softer.

"General!" the teacher said. "May I make a suggestion?"

"What is it?"

"Perhaps you could tell them the story of who the captured soldier is as a human being. Perhaps you could tell them the story of his family back home who's worried about him, and you could appeal to their sense of common humanity. After all, they have families back home who would be worried about them too if they were captured. Just a suggestion."

The general and his men looked at the teacher with an understanding that this kind of talk was a real part of war—partly because of the men and women they had studied in their class who had had things to say about war and about the whole idea of war—and they liked anything real like that, but they didn't know how to fit that into the game they were playing, not without ending it, and they went back to threats and demands, before retreating to make anew their plans of attack.

But even so, they had a look now like their teacher at least had done his job. They were playing at something that they would never want to *actually* be doing, and their teacher had reminded them of that, without interrupting the flow of the game. War was bad, even if the flow of their game wasn't bad, and as they ran, they all put that knowledge somewhere inside themselves, near where the bay and the sun and the trees were going.

The young man felt honored, and he couldn't say by what specifically, but it was mostly life. He felt honored to be a part of something that carried so much risk in every moment. Among men a man risked death, and among children he risked embarrassment. It was all right either way. The children he knew were going to grow up and see all that. It didn't mean that what they were under now was an illusion. They were being honest in their reaction to the nature around them. They seemed admitting of how they didn't know what else to do about the things that were bigger than them like the sand dunes and the sky, which was better than not admitting it and thinking of themselves as just as big. That was the real illusion. But aspiring to it was honest, and he knew that they'd seen him aspire to it through no war, and as long as they'd seen it, they could go on aspiring to it through war, because he knew that the effects of his aspiring would go past the park, and he knew that they would see that too.

BACK AND FORTH

There are two kinds of familiarity a man can have walking down the street. There is the familiarity of a place, of a place that is his place, and it is symbolized by the street itself, by its buildings, its stores and houses, its cracks in the sidewalk. It's a familiarity he gets tired of sometimes, and other times he thinks how nice it is to have his own little place in the world. He goes back and forth until he sees that he is a back-and-forth-er, and then the street becomes the home for a back-and-forth-er, and there is some symmetry at least in that.

There is another kind of familiarity that is more like familiarity with a condition. It is the familiarity a man feels walking down a street he has never walked down before. Yes, he thinks, walking down a street for the first time, just as I thought: man struggling—man trying to do his best with what he has been given, and a back-and-forth-ness everywhere, beginning with the back-and-forth between day and night and going from there. Sometimes it looks lousy, and sometimes it looks wonderful. But there is so much back-and-forth-ness that he sees that he is a back-and-forth-er wherever he is.

The essence of the story is written. What's left now is characters, each one embodying one of the two familiarities, and then each of those characters doing enough to qualify for a plot. Call the first one a family man. Give him a name that suggests routine but still respects his humanity. Give him a job in an office somewhere, a place he can walk to.

He could be from anywhere—Peru, Cambodia, Armenia—but a man can only be from one place at a time. Call him Rudolf Binz. He knows the walk from his house to his office like the back of his hand. He looks at the back of his hand, and he sees something old and weathered. It is his, though, and it carries memories, even as its oldness and weatheredness has come while walking up and down the same street. Nobody else knows exactly what it means to have been him, to have seen that street in all the different ways he has seen it, and every once in a while, he cannot escape the feeling that if he only could tell them, what a world it could be.

Think of the second man as belonging to that group of men carrying the majority of their possessions on their back. His vision is sharp for that which is very close or far away, but it is hazy for everything in between. Give him a name that connotes movement but evokes a childhood infused with more-conventional hopes and dreams. Call him Eric Slattery. He is convinced that there is nothing new under the sun, but he still has a lot of respect and affection for what is under the sun, especially when the sun is shining. And there are a million things he sees walking down a new street that are like an old friend, and like old friends do, he knows their grandeur and their foolishness both.

One day in the life of the world, a man named Rudolf Binz left his house and walked to the office where he had been walking for thirty-three years. Stopping in a cafe for a cup of coffee, he had a pleasant conversation with the young woman who worked there, just as he used to do with the young man who worked there before her and with the young woman who worked there before him. Coming back outside, he felt like the street was a little bit his and so, by extension, was the world.

Arriving in the city that morning by ship (cleanup crew) was a man named Eric Slattery. The first sound he heard in the new place was that of seagulls, and it took him back to seagulls in other cities, real and imagined. He couldn't remember which was which sometimes, and sometimes that was a nice feeling. Walking in no particular direction, he felt like the street was a little bit his and so, by extension, was the world.

Rudolf Binz began to whistle. Each step he took contained more than just today. It contained aspects of today—a clear sky, a light breeze, a report that had to be completed—but it contained his whole life too. If there had been a time when it had been useful to carry both of those equally while walking down the street, that time had been very short. The demands the world was making of him were being made today. Things like the cafe and the young woman who worked there helped him remember who he was. Even the places he only walked by, the places he had never stopped to notice, helped him remember who he was. They helped him remember that the relationship between himself and the world was a mutual one; there was back-and-forth-ness to it. A bank was on the corner where he turned down the street, and each time he saw it, he thought of money and his two children in college and bills in the near and distant future, but there were some mornings when he saw the pink light of the sunrise on its brick wall, and he felt that he had as much to say to the bank as it had to say to him.

Every day should start with a new city, thought Eric Slattery. It didn't seem like a lot to ask. Everything he saw seemed to deserve discovering. A bakery he stopped in to buy a loaf of bread for the day was a bakery, and it was the essence of a bakery. The one thing that he could say about his life was that it was honest. Every street he had ever walked down in every city, he had been looking for the same thing. And he was finding it and losing it, but at least he knew that. At least he knew that the man who was looking at any single thing was as important as the thing itself. Whether it was a fancy car or a beautiful woman or a thousand dollars, the man who was looking at them still mattered. I sure could use any one of those things, though, he thought. I sure would know what to do with them.

The street bent and shaped itself accordingly for each of the two men and their familiarity with it. It was just one day, but the familiarity that they each felt went back to a time when everything had been familiar and unfamiliar at once. A man wants to wake up in the morning knowing where he is. A boy had that knowledge no matter where he was, because wherever he was, he knew that he was a boy in it and that it was all right to wake up dreaming. That dream was with him, so whatever his struggle to make the world his, he knew that he was not alone in it. But a man has to make concessions to a boy, that those dreams he had were his own, that the time for dreaming was then. It is up to him to know where he is waking up in the morning, and it is good to have at least *something* familiar for that. It is only a starting place, but it is a place from which every possibility can start.

Eric Slattery sat down on a bench to eat a little of the bread he had bought. Nearby was a newspaper stand, and Rudolf Binz stopped there to buy a paper. The headlines gave shape and contour to his day. The names of the people doing great and scandalous things were names he knew, and they helped him remember who he was. He was a man who agreed with greatness and disagreed with scandal, and he could look at his own life and find confirmation of that, because even if it was hard to find the greatness, at least he did not find the scandal.

Eric Slattery looked over at him and thought, Ah, you already know what's in there. Eric already knew that *he* knew what was in there, but there was something about the man's face that made it seem like he knew it too. It was something alive in his face, more alive than anything the newspaper could reach.

Rudolf Binz noticed the man looking at him, and there was a way that the familiarity of the street and the familiarity of his day told him to look at a man eating his breakfast on a bench with his bag of possessions next to him, but before he could get to that, he saw the man's face, and he knew that if he were to leave it as what those familiarities said, he would be closing the discussion, and even though he didn't know what other familiarity he could have had with life, there was no reason to close the discussion.

He folded the newspaper and put it under his arm and went on his way, and Eric Slattery admitted that there was something nice about it, that even though he already knew what was in there, even though the newspaper had seemed like a part of a lie that was everywhere from the time he was a young man, there was something nice about a newspaper with a man walking down the street in the morning.

There was a back-and-forth inside them, and there was a back-and-forth outside them. There was a back-and-forth that they were a part of, and it was unlikely that any man had ever seen in its fullness how he was a part of it, except at the moment of life or at the moment of death. They didn't have to see it in its fullness, though, to know that they were in it with each other, that familiarity was what they both were after and what they both could provide. They each carried a world of familiarity in their face, and there were a million other things they carried in their faces, indications of the particular world that they had each become familiar with, but all it took was one thing from the world they shared, from the street they shared, which was the essence of the world and the street, because discovery was something shared almost by definition. Its thrill was in opening something up that others might see, even if it was only seen as indirectly as on the face of the man discovering it. Those men will see each other one day. They will see each other, and they will know that they are seeing each other for the first time, at a moment in their own back-and-forths and in the back-and-forth of the world, and they will know that man is at the center of their familiarity with the world, that the light of the sunrise and the sound of the seagulls matter because of what they can take back with them to tell him, which no amount of back-and-forth has ever found words for, but which no amount of familiarity with the street has ever made them stop looking for either.

SUNDAY IN THE PARK

There were Iranians for as far as the eye could see, if those eyes were those of thirteen-year-old Bahman Sohrabi, and the first thing he felt when he arrived at the park was that he was a blank piece of paper, and in this place he could be what he showed himself to be. Nobody had any expectations of him except for the expectations each had of him- or herself—to be a speaker of the language, an appreciator of the food and of the music and of nature, and a general participator in the whole thing. At school he found the spaces for a guy who did not want to be a participator in the whole thing right away. He found them in himself and in the school. But at the park he did not see those spaces. It was a park, for heaven's sake, so even if he saw them, they would still be beautiful.

It was something about the way Iranians looked in a park. It was a place everybody agreed on. The people didn't have any of the awkwardness they had in the daily transactions of life. The men looked able, and the women looked sure, and the children looked easy and happy. Bahman felt glad for all of it. He knew that they deserved it. He knew from watching his own mother and father, seeing who they were at home and seeing how they had to adjust out in the world. The trees and the grass and the park were a different story. Those things welcomed them back like the whole business of coming to America was a short trip, and they greeted each other like they had only been gone for a few days. It was part of the wonder of being among the first people to come to a place— they were mystified by the presence of a community, and yet they wanted to treat it like an everyday thing. At least in a park they were surrounded by evidence that mystification and the everyday went together.

Bahman carried a pot of rice to one of the picnic tables. His father carried a basket of fruit and a thermos of hot water for tea. Bahman liked the way his father and the other men did not become informal in their manner and appearance. They just changed the nature of their formality. A day at the park was still serious. An appreciation of the blue sky still required a reliance on tradition and custom. Something about their people made it seem as if they were always working. They were always attuned to the best way to do a thing. He had a respect for that, but he felt lost as well, because he almost never knew the best way to do a thing.

Right away he looked for a game. That was one place where he did know the best way to do a thing. He looked for a volleyball net, and once he found it, he looked to see who was playing to see how competitive it was. He did not want to act like the grass and the trees and the lake weren't important in themselves, but it was just the clarity of a game. He told the grass and the trees and the lake that he would come back to see them later, and he walked to the game.

His cousin Maryam's husband, Houshang, was there in the middle of it as always. He was playing barefoot and calling his friend Ghaffari "Professor" whenever he missed a shot.

"What happened, Professor? That was a good opportunity, Professor. . . . Bahman!" he said. "You are on our team."

A brief argument ensued, and Bahman smiled because he knew it was a joke—they were going to let him play. He jumped in the back corner and looked around to see who he could set the ball to. The first time he hit it, he hit it out, and there was a moment of teasing, but it was just a way to bring him into the game, and he needed to get a feel for things first. He looked at the team across the net from him as they got ready to serve. The team was made up of Ghaffari and two young women and two men close to his father's age. He knew them. He could look at them and know that he was seeing who they were, and he could listen to them and know that he was hearing who they were. It was not a way he always felt. It seemed like the closest he could come among people to the honesty of the sun coming through the trees.

What he liked about Iranians was the way they could care about the game and about everything else too. He did not have to wonder if he was the only one thinking of the sun coming through the trees. It was what they had woken up with. It was what they had all known about back when they decided to come here on a Sunday in the spring. The knowledge ran deep, and it meant that the expectation was high for a singular beauty inside all that.

I like those expectations, he thought. But he didn't know how he would live up to them except that for now he could live up to them in his movements on a volleyball court. He had a couple of plays, saves where nobody thought he could reach the ball, but he and the ball and the sun had their own understanding, and even his countrymen didn't know it until they saw it displayed.

After the game he walked back by himself. By himself was not by himself among Iranians. He could move among them easily, like a fish swimming in the sea. Walking by himself was a growing, opening-up thing, not a closing down of anything. He passed by a family speaking in Farsi about passing around the salad, and it went past them to make the park a growing, opening-up place, and maybe past that. What he should do, he thought, was remember this place all the time, especially at school, and bring its spirit with him because maybe the teachers and students didn't know. Maybe they didn't know that people could do this, that they could go to the park on a Sunday afternoon and let the world come to them. Maybe they could learn from people whose own country was far away. It wasn't a crazy thought. Everything had a little sadness to it when your own country was far away, and he didn't see anything wrong with everything having a little sadness to it, because everything *did* have a little sadness to it. It didn't matter to him what helped people to see it. It just happened that Iranians all had at least one thing.

He sat down at their table and ate of the *loobya polo* with yogurt. His father was talking with some other men under a tree. He did not have to hear them to know what they were saying: What was going to happen to the world? It was a question of what was going to happen to Iran in particular, but all of them were men whose world and whose country had been tied together for as long as they knew how to think. The men crossed their arms and looked at the ground and came in close to each other's faces to emphasize their points. Nobody thought of saying, It is a picnic—it is not the place for this kind of talk. Everybody knew it was exactly the place for it. There was nothing about a tree that looked like it wasn't the place for it. There was nothing about the sun and the grass that looked like that. Their formality made sense, because a man had always to be prepared for the most serious discussion he had inside him. He never knew when it was going to show up. And when men who were always prepared like that came together, it showed up as soon as they did.

His sister was sitting nearby, and he motioned toward the little girl in the family he'd passed by.

"Hey," he said, "why don't you go and become friends with her?"

"I don't want to," his sister said.

"Why not?" he said. "Look at her." He didn't understand why his sister didn't want to become friends with her. It seemed like the best part of being seven, the ease of making friends.

"I heard her say she likes horses," he said.

"No, you didn't."

"I was walking by, and she said, 'You know what I like more than anything? Horses.'"

"No, you didn't."

"It's okay. It's okay to be shy."

"I'm not shy!"

"Bahman!"

"Okay, sorry," he said. It was a fool's game trying to increase the amount of friendship in the world among seven-year-old girls. He stared philosophically at the men under the tree.

A soccer game was starting among some of the older boys. Bahman watched and wished it was basketball. The only thing he loved about soccer was the way it looked Iranian. He especially liked to watch the boys who had only recently come to America. They looked so comfortable when a soccer ball was on the grass, like all the trouble of having just come here was off them. He thought he had it rough, but those boys were only just learning English, starting at new schools at a time when American kids their age were applying to college. They knew how to look happy, though, and they let that happiness come out to each other in a way that he was not used to seeing boys do. He liked to think that some of that was in him, even though he seemed a long way from finding the place for it. He liked to think it was there.

"Do you see that tall boy with the glasses?" his mother said. "He has been here for a month. His brother was killed in the war."

He had known something was important about their presence in the park. A boy whose brother had been killed in the war with Iraq. That's what it was, Bahman thought. He felt relieved. It hadn't been just his imagination.

He knew that that sense of importance came from somewhere—the sad music in the people, the way he could see them trying to turn it into a music that was gladder, into laughter, into a serious discussion. And then sometimes they let the music be as sad as it wanted to be, which was usually too sad for him, but he still felt proud of them for being willing to do it. He couldn't admit that to anybody, including himself, but he could admit that the sadness came from somewhere.

He watched the boy and tried to see the war, but he couldn't. He felt as if he'd have to hate somebody to do it, either Iraqis for fighting or Iranians for fighting back and letting the boy's brother get killed, and he couldn't do either one. He felt bad for not being able to see the war that his country was fighting, but that didn't mean he didn't want things to turn out all right for the boy playing soccer.

His father came back and joined them. He poured himself a cup of tea. "I should learn my lesson," he said. "Talking about Iran with those men, whenever I do it, they speak wistfully of Iran before the revolution, as if it was some kind of paradise back then."

"It was a paradise if you had money," his mother said.

"Yes. And they had money."

Bahman listened and felt something very far from the disgust his father felt for the other men. If his father could look so worldly and dignified when he was talking with men he was disgusted with, how would he appear when he was talking with men he liked? Bahman had to hand it to Iranians. They had something very old about them, but then so did the trees they stood under to talk, which was why they could look like they belonged there. They could look like they belonged on the grass playing soccer when they had only been in America for a month.

He could look like he belonged here too. He could feel that way at least when they gathered in the park. There was a common language, beyond Farsi. It was a pace and a rhythm. It was a slowness, though sometimes it was a quickness too. He felt sure that he would someday be able to take it out to the world with him. It seemed like a long way off, but he didn't think it was only ever going to be for Sunday afternoons in the park.

Bahman watched the game, and past the field, up over the hill, he saw a family walking down toward everybody. They were fat. The father and the mother and the little boy were all fat. Bahman had never seen them before. He asked his father if he knew them.

"His name is Garousi," his father said. "He is a mechanic. I have heard he is a good mechanic."

Bahman watched them walk down the hill carrying their food and blanket. They were looking for a place to sit, for somebody they knew. If his father had heard that the man was a good mechanic, some of the men must have taken their cars to him. He hoped to hell that somebody would call out, "Hey, come on over here!" He thought of asking his father to do it, but he didn't. Bahman tried to watch the game and didn't watch as the father and the mother and the little boy circled the field and came back around in his family's direction. The father didn't look embarrassed, just a little curious that his friends hadn't shown up, though Bahman felt sure that he had seen some customers. He knew damn well that the man had seen some customers, and he watched the family lay out a blanket all the way over by the hill where they had started, and he thought furiously, knowing that he had just seen the one thing about the afternoon that was going to stay with him past anything else—us too, we do this too. In our language and all that, slowness and rhythm and all that, among the grass and the trees and the lake, we do this too.

THE BOOKSHELVES

On her shelves were books of many kinds and a picture of her grandmother who could not read. Each time she finished a book, she put it back on the shelf, and she looked at the picture of her grandmother, and she thought, It does not make me wiser than you. It does not make me more anything than you. It makes me in America and you in Iran. It makes me in the present and you in the past. That's all.

What this fellow Vygotsky is saying, Grandmother, is very interesting. And Friere too. You would've liked them. They loved children, first of all. And bell hooks, I think you would've really liked her. She's not afraid of anything. They're only doing what you would've done.

There was a man named Karl Marx. I think you would've liked him too. You don't know how much your son who is my father liked him. I could write another book about that.

There are so many of them that I wish you knew. It's not just the ones who tried to say this is how the world really works. It's the ones who told stories and sang poems. You would've liked all of them.

She liked the way her grandmother's picture sat at the top of the bookshelf. She loved her books, but they were only books. They were not everything. There was something about her grandmother's life that could never fit in a book. All of them could say *something* about it. Or when she was reading, she would understand something about her grandmother's life that was true. But none of them could get at the whole thing. And among all the books she liked, the best would've admitted that; all the writers from all over the world from the beginning of books sat on her shelves and admitted that—Dostoyevsky and Du Bois and Marquez and Gibran and Morrison—at their best, they all admitted that they couldn't get at the whole of the life of her grandmother who could not read, and she thought that if she were ever able to join them, with a book of her own that would go on the shelves, she would want it to be under the picture of her grandmother so that there wouldn't be any confusion as to what came from what and she would be able to say to her grandmother, you would've liked me too.

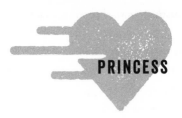

PRINCESS

The whole thing is lousy to look back on because she would call herself a princess in those days when we first met and I wouldn't know what she was talking about. I didn't have any idea what she was talking about. I had a mind that was half-white in those days, so when she called herself a princess, I figured she was looking for a guy who was a prince, and to me that sounded like captain-of-the-football-team kind of stuff. If she was looking for a guy who thought of himself as a prince, that wasn't me. I had just moved to the city, and I was more interested in paupers than princes. I would stop on Market Street and talk to the guys asking for change and try to understand how they had gotten there. There was a sadness in the world, and I was interested in going into it. I was twenty-two years old, and I was trying to take on as much of it as I could. I didn't know what else to do. I didn't know that a woman could call herself a princess and still be trying to do that too. The other half of my mind was Iranian, only it was in the Iran that we had left, and the presence of royalty had been the reason we had left; it had been the reason my father had been imprisoned when he was young, and one of the first understandings of the world I had as a boy was that a king was someone who believed that he could rule over everyone else for no apparent reason, and that trickled its way down to princes and princesses and left me feeling like I wanted nothing to do with the whole thing.

Nobody expects you to learn about black people when you come to America from another country. Nobody expects you to learn why a black girl would call herself a princess, why there has to be a word for the notion that she is not ugly for being black, not unfeminine for being black, not unlikely to be the source for a man's heart riding out beyond what it has known for being black. The word covers it about as well as any word could.

Look, I said in those days, if you're looking for princes, they're out there. I've seen them. They're driving expensive cars and wearing stylish clothes. They're waking up on Sunday mornings at Lake Tahoe and in Napa Valley. They're not waking up in the Tenderloin of San Francisco wondering what the hell they're going to write. Me, I'm just hanging on. I'm just hanging on to literature and children and the crowds in the evening on Powell Street and long walks to the bay, looking at everybody and everything, really. It's everything, but still I'm just hanging on. The funny thing is that I like it this way. I never expected any different. But if there's some way to have it be everything and have me just hanging on and still be a prince about it, I sure as hell don't know what that is.

The thing that I didn't know and nobody told me was that nothing about being a princess meant that she had to place herself above anybody. There was nothing that couldn't be trying to spread itself out for free. It was a very democratic kind of princesshood. I just didn't know. Instead I would get to thinking about my father in prison when she talked of being a princess or about the men on Market Street asking for change, and everything would turn out no good. There was a lot I didn't know. But a young man of twenty-two is looking for a way to understand his father and men asking for change, and I jumped at the chance to feel like I was on their side. The crazy thing was that she was on their side too. I knew that she was on their side too, so when I put myself over there as a place to hide from the princess stuff, it felt like a very small and isolated corner, instead of the big and open space it should be.

A man draws lines—I did anyway—and when my father told me about being in prison when I was a boy, I drew the lines to match the prison bars he saw, and I put myself on one side and kings and queens and anything that had anything remotely good to say about them on the other, and I went along like that carrying those lines with me in America for a long time, long enough to forget I was carrying them, and then a woman came along who knew all about lines, who knew all about them from being a woman and from being black, and knew about being more than someone carrying lines around with her too, and when I look back on the whole thing, it's pretty lousy to think about, because I can see how she was telling me about being a princess because she saw some part of me as a prince. But I couldn't do it. I couldn't figure out how to look in two directions at once, in the direction of paupers and in the direction of princes, so I stuck to looking at paupers and saying to hell with princes. I held on to that line and kept it with me until I couldn't live on one side of it anymore. To live like that wasn't helping anyone, and I came around to understanding that I could look at at least everybody. Everybody was who I had around me, and I could at least look at each person and see what there was on either side of that line that I could use to make who I wanted to be.

And I guessed that was something that she had done a long time ago. It was a little bit of where grace came from in her, not having those lines inside her, not having them be bigger than her at least. She saw that those lines were not hers; they had been imposed on her by men who needed lines, so why should she hold on to them like they were? And there was princesshood in that. I caught on to it too late, but there was princesshood in that grace and that freedom and that willingness to give. But like I said, nobody expects you to learn about black people when you come to America from another country. Nobody asks you about it when you take the U.S. citizenship test. I was asked about the Korean War and the Constitution, but not about Nat Turner and Malcolm X. Asking that would be a start. And then if they really wanted to do something worthwhile with it, they could ask why it's always different when a black girl calls herself a princess from when a white girl does it.

If I could tell her now, I'd want to tell her that I'm sorry, that I was looking for a way to carry my feelings about my father in prison, about the men on Market Street asking for change, and I didn't know that there was a way of living that had so much poetry to it, that had *had* to have so much poetry to it, that shining was a kind of survival, and that a princess was a girl who had stayed living, who had kept her own heart, who could look in any direction and see the humanity that was there because she had refused to give up any of her own, and it's just a whole lot better to let words mean the best of what they can mean, instead of using them to fight old battles that I can't even win, and for what it's worth, I certainly wish I'd known that back then.

WHY THE RABBIT LOOKS
PITYINGLY UPON THE DONKEY

(An Iranian American Folktale from Long Ago)

In Farsi, the word for "donkey" is *khar* and the word for "rabbit" is *khargoosh*, which means "donkey ears." Way back in the old days when words were still relatively new, the rabbits got together and started asking why they should be named after the donkey. Why couldn't they have a name of their own?

"You don't see a *kerm* (worm) get named after a *mar* (snake)," one said, "though their bodies bear a resemblance."

"That's true," another said. "You don't see a *sag* (dog) get named after a *rooba* (fox), though they look even more alike."

"You're right," the first one said. "I don't think our ears even look that much like a donkey's. Ours are much more attractive."

To this last point all the other rabbits concurred, as they were generally vain animals.

So all the rabbits went to see Old Allah, who'd made all the animals and named them. The real reason that Old Allah had given them the name *khargoosh* was that they were one of the last animals he'd made, and he was tuckered out after making and naming animals all day. He'd noticed their long ears looked like the donkey's and called them *khargoosh* and that was that. But he also remembered that in his tiredness he'd accidentally spilled an extra dose of vanity upon them, so he was ready for them when they came.

The rabbits told Old Allah that he'd done a fine job in making them, but that such fine-looking animals deserved a better name than anything that carried a reference to the donkey and its ears.

Old Allah heard them out, and when they were finished, he said, "You ever taken a long look at a donkey?"

Before they could respond, he said, "A more pathetic-looking animal I could not make. Not graceful like an *asb* (horse), not powerful like a *nar* (bull). Not good for anything except dragging stuff around for the *ensans* (humans)."

The rabbits looked at each other, as it seemed like Old Allah was making their case for them.

"Do you know the one source of pride this poor, pathetic animal has?" Old Allah said.

The rabbits did not know.

"Its one source of pride is that the beautiful and magnificent *khargoosh*, due to a merely passing resemblance to its ears, is named after it. It is the one thing keeping the poor old fellow from the abyss of despair. Whenever it sees a *khargoosh* and remembers its connection to its name, it thinks that maybe there is a little hope in this life after all."

The rabbits were quiet and deeply moved. Given their beauty and magnificence, they couldn't say they were altogether surprised, though.

Since then, whenever a *khargoosh* encounters a *khar*, it looks on it with great pity, remembering that the merely passing resemblance of their ears is its one source of pride. As donkeys are not very expressive animals and so can be said to be feeling whatever a viewer seems to think they are feeling, the rabbit would swear that it sees the spark of hope in its eyes.

FLOWER-LIKE

I did not have a Lost Generation
or a Beat Generation, but I had a group of girls that I coached on a basketball team, and I didn't have to talk to the team about art because when
we warmed up before a game outside the gym, the sky was something
that we could certainly understand *somebody* painting, especially an artist.
We happened to be dribbling and passing and shooting, but we might be
painting someday, or looking at a painting, or looking at another kind
of art, and we would certainly want to be doing that with our best selves.
We were dribbling and passing and shooting with our best selves, and
each of us knew that we were doing two things then: we wanted the ball
to go where it was supposed to go, and we wanted ourselves to go where
we were supposed to go. And life was a thing where we wouldn't always
have a ball in our hands, but we could always have a say in where we were
going, even if it was only where we were going inside ourselves. That
was the biggest place to go of all, and that was the biggest thing that I
wanted to teach the team: that there were undiscovered places inside
each of them, and basketball had helped me discover mine, and I wasn't
claiming to know theirs, just that they were there. And plenty of the undiscovered places were still in me; the best part of living was believing
that there was always more undiscovered than discovered, and I wanted
to show them that the real beauty of a team lay in discovering together.
And the beautiful part was that those places were already inside them,

before they learned a thing about basketball. I wanted to take the people that they already were and add basketball. For some of them, that meant adding detail to their basketball knowledge, and for some of them it meant introducing things for the first time. But they were all already in possession of most of the things that make a good basketball team: they had a readiness for art and for art's capacity to give them something to aim for in how they lived and moved, and in turn they could see that how they lived and moved went beyond the drawing class and the poetry class and the chorus in its creativity.

We would drive to different parts of the city for games, and inasmuch as we were in San Francisco, along the way we might pass something beautiful—a mural or a park or scene on the street. I would try to suggest to the team that the passing beauty was not unrelated to how we ought to play. Sometimes I would only get as far in my suggesting as thinking it, and I hoped that the team would realize that my silence was a thoughtful one. Other times I would tell the team members directly that they should step on the court with their minds in the same place as they were at the beginning of art class. Only they should leave a little of their minds in the place it was at the beginning of math class. That was the part of following directions and remembering what we had practiced. If they could do that and still bring to the court something of what the world was saying at its most poetic, I figured that was pretty much genius. I didn't know what else it could be. It was funny how long a good pass would stay with me as evidence that it was an artist's world. It was funny because when I tried to think of other writers who along the way put their hearts into coaching girls' middle-school basketball, I couldn't come up with any. I thought and thought and came up with none.

Which just meant that the faith that it was a good thing for a writer to do along the way had to come from me. Nobody had to know that there were principles that I tried to bring to the team that had come to me at my writing desk. The girls themselves did not have to know. They just had to put the principles into practice. Even if I had had a Lost Generation or a Beat Generation, I still couldn't have brought all of who I was to those circles. I couldn't necessarily have brought all my feelings about a full-court press to them.

I didn't want the girls to feel the way that I did about basketball necessarily either, but I wanted them to feel that way about *something*. In the meantime, we had basketball. For me it had been the thing that was beyond sarcasm. And when I set out to write in a way that was beyond sarcasm, I knew a little bit of what that should feel like.

That was the part of the game that they excelled at, the part that went beyond sarcasm. The ones who could shoot and the ones who couldn't, the ones who could dribble and the ones who couldn't—it was true for all of them. And that was the start of everything we would become as a team. Don't see the miss, I thought, when one of their shots bounced off the rim or the backboard. See the heart. Address the shot. Address the knees and elbow and feet and balance and fingertips. But see the heart. See it contained in the arc of the path of the ball. Try to love basketball, not just the shots that go in.

Let them know that there was one place in the world where effort was always rewarded. Its reward was the chance to learn more about effort. You had to trust that they were making their own individual discoveries. After a practice, I would measure our progress by how the city looked. It didn't have to look beautiful; it only had to look like a canvas. If it did that, then I would know that the two hours we'd spent in the gym hadn't taken anything *away* from life. I didn't know if it meant that we would win our next game or not. Try to love basketball more than winning, I would think.

The whole thing was as quiet as an artist working, in truth. That was what made it so funny and surprising in the last minutes of a close game when the whole thing seemed like a loud and boisterous affair. It would surprise me every time. It wasn't the volume of the noise; it was its nature. I actually would have the girls practice yelling myself. I would have somebody stand at half-court with the ball, and I would have the girls stand under the basket and yell for the ball, to practice calling loudly for it when they were open. But it was quiet because it was purposeful.

It was the same thing with aggressiveness. It was a very private and inward and personal thing. Nobody knew what the experiences were that a player was drawing her aggressiveness from. She did not have to tell anyone, and maybe she did not know herself. Have those secrets, I thought. They can come out on a basketball court for now, and they may come out in other ways later. I hope they come out in the ways you want them to come out.

It was a heart-centered thing, and that was why I never could show it. I didn't want them to know that the importance of a ball going in the basket or not depended on a heart. I didn't want them to know that the importance of a team winning a game or not depended on a heart. I didn't want them to see that I had once had a time when my heart couldn't rise to meet the importance of those things. They did not always think of a heart as something separate from themselves, and I liked it that way. So I would dance around it and make suggestions here and there that their hearts were theirs as much as vice versa, which was okay because I liked dancing.

There was the time I saw Janie Eliezer crying after making a mistake at the end of a close game we lost.

"You okay?" I said. I put my hand on her head.

She nodded.

That was all I said, but I felt like she knew that I meant it was okay either way. It was okay to cry, and it was okay to stop crying. Her tears were beautiful, and her effort to fight her tears was beautiful too.

There was Cynthia Vasquez. She and I had an understanding. If she missed her first shot, I would tell her to keep shooting. She was new to basketball, but she was not new to confidence. She would nod as she went back down the court as if she knew I was talking to the confidence she already had, as if we knew each other from way back.

It was like that all the time, all of us letting each other know that we were on each other's side as people, and building from that to be on each other's side as a basketball team. I had to laugh sometimes because there was poetry in running sprints when everybody believed in running sprints. I had to laugh because there had been a notion when I was a kid that the boy running sprints on the basketball team and the boy reading poetry were somehow far apart, when in fact they were the same boy.

That was a wonderful thing about coaching those girls. Basketball was something they played, not something they possessed. When they put their uniforms on at the end of the school day, it was because that was what they wore to play basketball. Somebody else might be going to a violin lesson, and that was just as fine.

It was the kind of basketball I wished I'd had—something democratic and shared and made of a love for basketball that was independent of one's ability at basketball. I knew that ability was still important, but the idea was that basketball was everybody's. Nobody had to have it any less for anybody to have it any more. We lost our first few games of the season, but I wanted the girls to know that basketball was still theirs as much as it had been at the beginning of the season. It could still be a home. They had to think of it as a home in order to play comfortably. It might mean finding some new definitions of comfort. Still those definitions would draw upon worlds those girls already contained. They already knew about kindness and thoughtfulness and patience. I just wanted them to know that who they were was enough. It was a matter of bringing all of who they were out.

If you wanted to achieve something, there was not a lot of fanfare in it. There were no crowds or applause or celebrations during the *process*. It was even a lonely thing sometimes because nobody could really say what it was that made us want to be a good team. Little by little we began to be able to look at each other and see our achievement. The best part of it was that we had a notion that it was inside of something else, something that went back to a time that was before the team and before basketball. It went back to a time when our best selves were our only selves. That was when we knew that basketball was the thing to love more than the shots that went in, more than winning. We knew it naturally, and we had been right. Whatever we learned and did after that was only to be added to it.

The smell of the concrete when we practiced outside, the angle of the sun and the shadows, the cold air in the afternoon, they were all consequential to our efforts as a team. How were you going to be in the moment of basketball if you weren't in the moment of the world first? We wanted our love of basketball to be a love, not a need and not an escape. I thought about how I did not want my writing to be an escape, for me or for anybody reading it. I wanted to write and to have somebody read what I wrote and to come back to the world with an eagerness for it, not with a reluctance toward it, like how I first learned how I loved Chekhov: I was reading a book of his stories in a bookstore, and when I looked up from a story, a husband and wife were talking beside me. I don't remember what they were talking about, but their conversation seemed completely Chekhovian.

You can make things your story, I told those girls at every practice. You will see a girl dribbling hard to the basket, and you may feel like a character in her story. You are not a character in her story. Neither is she a character in yours, but you have as much right to yours as she does to hers. What it means, though, to have a story is to want things.

We talked a lot about wanting things because we knew there were such things as acquisitiveness and greed, and we wanted to know the difference between wanting and those. We wanted to know how we were still being like flowers when we wanted, because we had learned something flower-like about so many other parts of the game. We finally came on the difference together. It was in wanting without diminishing what we already had. So when we won the semifinal playoff game, we set about trying to want in the right way.

To see how much we wanted was frightening. We had wanted such simple, little things at the beginning of the season. And now we were in a position to want the league championship. It was frightening to want something seemingly infinite after having done our wanting in small, daily increments. Still, it was a small, daily increment of its own, along with being infinite. And we had not been heedless of infinity along the way. We had been playing with principles that went beyond the small, daily moment because they went beyond basketball. They went to how we understood each other. I don't know everything about you, we told each other, but I see you trying. That was what I had told people back when I had wondered how I was going to stay among them. I had to call them strangers first. I had to acknowledge the distance before I could look for what bridged it. The girls did not try to let their personal friendships be the thing that held us together. They knew they needed something more universal and steady. They knew they needed something new.

It was being seen. You only had to see someone to see them trying. You had to have a quietude somewhere in you that let you know that being seen was enough. I wasn't asking that that quietude be all of who they were. They could be a million other things, and they were. But I did want them to love that part of themselves and to be proud of it. And they got so good with that part that they could even be generous with it.

At the end of the championship game, we were ahead by three points with nine seconds to play. The other team had the ball and called a time-out. In the huddle I told the girls that our goal was to prevent the other team from shooting an open three-pointer. To do that, we would play man-to-man defense. We had been playing zone defense all season.

I paused as I said it because they were not men; they were girls, and they had every reason to be proud to be girls, and there were plenty of other places where they wouldn't be given reason to be proud to be girls, and I wondered if I should call it girl-to-girl defense because they deserved to be called the thing they were when they were on the court being who they were. I could even say it nervously or awkwardly, and they would see my trying more than my nervousness or awkwardness.

But I didn't do it. The moment was too serious for nervousness or awkwardness, and I forgot that you had to be in the world before you could be in a basketball game. As soon as I said it, they looked at me with a certainty and sympathy. I could see it in their faces: you could have called it girl-to-girl defense. You could've even said it nervously or awkwardly. It wouldn't have taken away from the seriousness of the moment. It would've only added to it. Even if we'd smiled or laughed, it would've only added to it.

I saw them put that certainty and sympathy away somewhere inside themselves and go to the court and play beautiful girl-to-girl defense and steal the ball to win the game. Everything was rosy and full of flowers until a little time passed, and I felt foolish for not calling it girl-to-girl defense, though I felt proud that they'd given me a chance, and I could still learn from the way they'd put it aside and played it.

THE NARRATOR

It wasn't strange when she said it somehow. It came within the flow of her conversation. When they first met, when she knew it was coming, she would say, "Now he is going to ask me for my phone number." The men would be charmed. They would feel like they were inside a story. And then on their first night together, saying goodbye, it would be the same thing—"Now he is going to kiss me."

Then later: "Now he is going to come into my room."

"Now he is going to kiss my neck."

"Now he is going to undress me."

It was very funny and charming and witty. The benefit of it for her was that if she could give them a story, she would not have to tell them hers. She did not like to tell them that she had been married at twenty-two and divorced at thirty-two because that had been a last-gasp effort at something, and if they knew how much of a last gasp it was, if they knew how close she had been to saying good-bye to people altogether when she had gotten married . . . well, they wouldn't want to hear it, that's all.

As long as she told the story, she could tell herself the last part, "Now he is going to leave," and she would believe it.

That was how it went until she met a man who told her on their first night not to narrate their time together.

"I am not 'he,'" he said.

"Of course you are," she said.

"No," he said. "If I am he, then you are she, and you are not she. You are you."

"I am a woman," she said. "Do you know how much time in a day people look at me as she?"

"I am not people."

"It's not so easy as that. You can't just announce that you're not people and let it go at that."

He smiled. "You called me you."

"I said it in anger. Doesn't that bother you?"

"I'd rather be a you in anger than a he any day."

"I wouldn't. Being a you is terrible."

"Sure it is. But it's wonderful too. We are all he's and she's enough as it is. Walking down the streets downtown, we're all he's and she's."

"No. Walking down the streets downtown, we're barely anything."

"Well, I don't know about that. But what about when you're walking and you see somebody you know? You say, 'It's you!'"

"I don't," she said. "When I see them, I think, It's them."

He studied her face to see if she was just being charming.

"This is going to be a climb, isn't it?" he said.

"What?"

"To become a you."

"It's not so bad to be a he," she said.

"It's second best."

"Second best is not so bad."

He looked at her and smiled sadly.

"It's a long way from best," he said.

"Best is overrated. People should be happy with second best."

"They are. Until they have a chance at best."

"Now you're overstepping your bounds. How do you know what you have a chance at?"

"I know it because you're admitting yourself that it's second best. That's what's sad about it."

"I have a good reason to be glad with second best!"

"I didn't say you don't have a good reason. I just said it was sad. What is the reason?"

"I don't need you to feel sorry for me."

"All right, I won't feel sorry for you. What is the reason?"

"I don't like to say it because it sounds ordinary."

"There are no ordinary reasons for this kind of thing."

"Yes, there are. It is ordinary. It happens all the time. I was married when I was young, and I was divorced after ten years."

"For what it's worth, I think that's a great reason."

"It's ordinary. It's boring and ordinary."

"It isn't."

"Yes, it is."

"If it was ordinary, then I would have come across some other women who did that. You're the first woman I've ever known to narrate me."

"It's not just you I've narrated. Don't go thinking you're special."

"Look," he said, "I'm not saying it isn't charming. It's very charming. But I'm interested in who you are past charming."

"That's a very rude thing to say. How would you like it if I said that I was interested in who *you* are past charming?"

"That would be all right."

"Well, I don't want to know who you are past charming. Once we do that, there's no going back. Let's stick to charming. Charming can be wonderful, don't you think?"

"Charming can be wonderful with people who aren't anything past it. You are."

"How do you know I am anything past it? Maybe I'm not anything past it at all."

He looked at her sadly again.

"Do you really think this is a feasible way to be?"

"Feasible? Who do you think you are?"

"I'm no he."

"Yes, you are."

"No," he said, "I'm not. I've got nothing against him, whoever he is. I'm sure he's a perfectly nice fellow. But he's not me."

She looked so angry with him that he thought she might kiss him.

"Now she is going to kiss me," he said.

"Stop it!"

"Now she is going to put her arms around me."

"Stop it!"

"Not so fun, is it?"

"Don't do that. Don't rub it in."

"I'm sorry."

"It's not *such* a bad thing," she said.

"No, it's not. But it is second best."

"It's only our first night together."

"I know. But we can each be a you to each other right away."

"Maybe you can. I can't."

"I think you can. It's all right if it's an angry you. But not he. I've been a he all day. Out of the hundreds of thousands of people in this city, almost all of them saw me as he today, which is fine. I expect that from them. I don't expect it from you."

"You only just met me."

"Still, I don't expect it."

"I don't know if you should be expecting or not expecting anything."

"I do. I expect you to admit there's *always* something past charming."

"All right. There is. But can we stick to charming for tonight?"

"Sure. But no narration. No he's and she's. We can stick to you's and still be charming."

"I don't think I can."

"Sure you can. Forget the narrator. We don't need her. She deserves a rest anyway. She's been working hard. I can tell. Let her go off with the narrator in me. Let them go sit over there. Let them have a drink and narrate to each other all they want. We'll sit here and be you's to each other."

"Can they sit not too far away?"

He laughed.

"Sure. They can sit at the next table. We'll even wave to them halfway through."

"All right," she said. "Just over there?"

"Yes."

They both looked over at the next table.

"They make a nice couple, don't you think?"

"Yes," she said. "A little chatty, though."

He laughed.

"I'm sure they have a lot to catch up on."

"Yes," she said, "I think you're right."

They talked for three-and-a-half hours, until the place closed down.

"Can we bring them?" she said as they were leaving.

"I'd like to. I really would. There's only one problem. They left a while ago. They said to say good-bye."

"Oh, no."

"I'm afraid so."

"Let's find them."

"I don't think they want to be found. Anyway, she said to tell you that she will catch up with you later. She said she's not going away forever. But she said she thought it would be good for her to live her own life for a while. She thought it might be good for you to do the same."

"She said all that?"

"Yes. I think it was when you were in the bathroom."

EVERY MAN A SHOWMAN

Maybe it's the last thing that goes, a man's performance, which is nothing other than him. It's his walk into a room where he will be seen as less than a man, where the humanity of his movement is undeniable, so they will say, All right, he is a boy then, because performance is a boy's world. It is comical because the show started before he walked into the room; it started when he woke up in the morning, and before that it started when he was born. Why would anybody want to draw a thick black line between the boy and the man anyway, except for fear? Watch me dance on that line, a man says. You've never seen anybody move like this, if for nothing else than you've never seen this moment of the world before. The show is what's real. That moment when the curtain goes down and the audience walks out, that moment is a lie.

I'd always wanted to show others that that moment is a lie, until finally the only way to show them was to not go to movies anymore. And then the show opened up, and I could move through the world letting each man know that he had an audience member in me, and my only encouragement was that he make his performance true. As long as it was true, it was good. As long as he knew he was speaking from a stage, he was believing in his audience, and I learned in high school how Mr. Fyodor Dostoyevsky said that we are all responsible for all, and man as a showman is just exercising his responsibility one person at a time. He knows he can't get to everybody all at once, but if he carries his performance with him all the time, then he has something *for* everyone when they meet. I've seen it come out in desperation, but every man feels it more desperate to do nothing, or realizes it later, when he goes home and thinks, This sorrow is not just mine; it is everybody's, and I am done with acting like it's any different.

If you laugh along with the joke, it means you know where the joke came from, and the man who told it writes it down in his memory, as proof to himself that it is a public sorrow, not only shared but out in the open. It is *already* out in the open, so there is no genius in the discovery of that, only in the aligning of the public feeling with his private self. Everything he is by himself is building up to the public moment, and if he is smart, he's a little bit of an audience for himself when no one else is around. Get a load of this guy. Thinking he can do anything. He's a live one all right.

Somebody's already wondered like hell about him through the course of a day, namely, himself, so by the time the evening rolls around, he can roll with it. He can sit back like this is his world, and for all practical considerations, it is. This is his world that's got him by the back of the neck, but a man can still dance as long as his feet are free.

I stood outside one of the largest banks in the world and listened as the security guard told me, "You're crazy if you think I keep my money in there."

It was a warm evening in San Francisco.

"How do you think they got so big?" he said.

"Good point."

"I like things simple. A little money. A little music when you go home. A little time with your woman."

"Sounds wonderful," I said.

"It is wonderful. So why do we make it so hard? Why do we think a man has to have a mansion and a sailboat and a different woman every day of the week?"

"Ask the guy who owns this bank," I said.

"That's right. That's what it is. Somebody at the top says this is how it is. This is how it has to be. I don't *want* to be the guy at the top. I want to not worry about who's on top."

Just then a man came out of the bank. He was tall and wore sunglasses. He knew the security guard.

"They got me this time, Danny," he said.

"What'd I tell you? How'd they get you?"

"Foreclosing my place."

The guard shook his head. "I'm ashamed to be protecting this place."

The setting sun was shining beautifully off the man's sunglasses. Whatever had happened, I knew he didn't deserve to lose his house.

"Now get this," the guard said. "This same bank, when *they* need money, when *they* find themselves coming up short at the end of the month, where do they go?"

The man in the sunglasses smacked me on the shoulder. "Where do they go?" he asked.

He was putting on a show. I had heard the guard perfectly well the first time. I was standing next to him. But the man had just lost his house, and he saw a chance for a show. I understood.

"They walk right up to the government. They walk right up to the president."

"To the president," the man said, smacking me on the shoulder. I laughed. It was partly a comedy too. The man subtly fed off the laughter of his audience, like a great actor.

"They walk right up to the president and they say, 'Mr. President, we're a little short. We could really use your help.' And does the president say, 'All right, well, here's what I can give you'? No, he does not."

"No, he does not," the man said. Smack.

They were in a rhythm now. I tried to remember shows I'd seen where a character with a small role did his part admirably. That was what they needed from me. Each smack was directed toward a world the man wanted to love but had not made it easy for him to do so.

"Do you know what the president says? He says, 'How much do you need?'"

"How much do you need," the man said. He did not have a smack for me that time. He tried but there was nothing behind it. But I did something funny. I jerked back like there was. He was going to need showmanship when he left the bank. He was going to need it when he got home and saw the house he wasn't going to be able to keep anymore, and I wanted him to know that I was on his side for that.

A boy knows that he is a show as he is. He knows that he is worth marveling at, because he knows that none of the ugliness of the world is his doing. When he grows up, his show is a way to say hello to the boy. He is going to say hello to him one way or another, so he might as well be the show he intends to be.

My own show was believing. It was as real a show as there was. I used to look around among the audience when I was a boy and know that there was a great show happening there too. Now I had a chance to demonstrate that I had been right. It didn't matter if anybody believed it or not, any of the people walking by. They would know it when I was *their* audience too.

He was going to be all right. That's how it felt there outside the bank with the sun going down. We couldn't make another appointment for a showtime together, but the three of us had each had our show seen and acknowledged. What was important was that we would each be carrying our show with us wherever we went.

"Where are you going to go?" the guard said.

"I'll go to my brother's. He lost his job, but he's got his place. I still got my job at least."

He started walking away, looking back at us once, as if to say he had another smack for me if there was anything else, and then turned and left.

I rubbed my shoulder, but I didn't say anything about it. The guard didn't ask. He stared straight ahead. I got the message. It would've broken up the act. It didn't matter if it was one minute later or three days later or ten years. The show was the thing. You respected a man's performance, and you especially respected it when he needed it most.

Anyway, the guard was protecting a place he did not believe in. He had his own show going, from the time he woke up in the morning. There were men who told each other silently that they would keep each other's show going. I felt honored that they had included me in it. It didn't mean they weren't thinking of a time when they wouldn't need it, when a man would not have to protect a bank he did not believe in or lose his home because of the fine print. They *were* thinking of that time. They had just decided that the show was what was going to carry them there. And maybe when the numbers got into the hundreds and thousands, they didn't need it then. Maybe there was enough sincerity there as it was. But when it came to one man talking to another man on the street and wanting to show that love and decency are still on the table, that they are just as much a part of the daily exchange as the money transaction, I couldn't argue with their logic.

"He'll be all right," the guard said, staring straight ahead.

I nodded.

"You know, I've only talked with him a couple of times, but I probably know him better than anybody in the bank."

"I'm sure you do."

"You know what I think sometimes? I think of how if somebody were to try to rob this bank, I'd stop him. That's my job. But then you know what I'd like to do? I'd like to make everybody in the bank listen to the story of how he ended up robbing a bank. I'd like to make everyone sit down and listen. They're all nice people in there, but they don't know these stories. They don't know it's not something that just happens one day all of a sudden."

"Hell," I said, "I wish that was part of your job description."

We had a good laugh about that one. We laughed that our show extended out to people we didn't know and to their stories. It made me feel like the important thing about a man's performance was not how many people would see it in his lifetime. There would always be more who didn't than who did anyway. The important thing was how many people were *included* in his performance, and I felt thankful for the soreness in my shoulder to help me remember it for today.

DON'T FORGET ABOUT EGYPT

It was a joke his father and his father's brothers and their friends liked to use when they were entering a conversation. They were men who liked to talk and who liked to talk about politics and who looked so at home talking about politics that the boy would wonder where that home was. They looked like American men talking about sports, only there was more—more heights and depths of emotion, more putting their arms around each other, more slowness in listening to another man's heart coming out.

"Don't forget about Egypt," a newcomer would say. "What is the issue at hand?" It went back to London, to the hotel his father and his uncles had run there for Iranian students. There was a Turk who stayed there for a few weeks who wanted very much to participate in the big discussions they had after dinner. He just didn't know enough to do it, so one night he said, out of the blue, "Don't forget about Egypt. Egypt is strong too."

The men would be speaking of Iran and their hopes for it and of men there, alive or dead, who were doing great things if they were alive and who had once done great things if they were dead, and the boy would still be thinking of the Turk. He couldn't help it. The Turk was the one consistent part of all the discussions. He had been there through all the twists and turns. The boy felt so sorry for him that he didn't fully believe everything they said afterward about Iran having no more poverty and no more kings. He didn't want to be a man who talked about those things if laughing about the Turk was part of it. He didn't want to be an American man talking about sports, either, so he wasn't sure which way to go.

One afternoon in the summer he came inside from the yard where the men stood talking and slammed the door.

"What happened?" his mother asked.

"I feel bad for the Turk."

"What Turk?"

"The one who said, 'Don't forget about Egypt.'"

His mother thought back. "That was ten years ago."

"I know," the boy said. "So why do they keep talking about him?"

His mother didn't know what to say. She knew that it was a way to remember a time, but that didn't mean anything to the boy. The Turk was very much alive to him, somewhere in the world, because he was a boy.

That night she told the boy's father about it.

"That Turk!" he said, laughing. "Remember him? 'Egypt is strong too.' What a thing to say!"

"Well, he doesn't like it."

"What does he not like?"

"He thinks you are making fun of him."

"We are. But he is not in the room with us."

"That doesn't matter to him."

"But he was a baby when we had that hotel."

"That also doesn't matter to him."

The father smiled. He liked anything new, and this was new for him. It was new for him each day to find out that he was a father and that he was a father to a boy who liked to sit and listen to men talking and know what they had to say. He took it to mean that the boy was a little ahead of boys who were running around causing trouble, but he heard a thing like this, and he wondered if the boy was a little behind them. If that was the case, it was all right. He had already accepted that it was a crazy thing to try to understand the boy, at least in the way that he was used to trying to understand that which came from him as being his.

But he wondered what was going to happen to a boy who couldn't take a little joking. A lot worse was going to be coming his way. Either he was not going to be able to handle it or he was going to be able to handle all of it and then some. He was glad that the boy was getting some practice early. He had not gotten practice in that kind of thing when he was a boy, but that was all right. He thought about being on the other side, about being the one whose words made a boy angry at the world. It was a funny place to be. He laughed. If he hadn't been so sure about the fire inside him, he would have been upset at the boy's fire coming out toward him. But he loved that poor Turk, wherever he was. That hapless Turk. They all loved him. They wanted to remember him because it was in their part of the world that a man would be embarrassed not to be part of a political discussion. In America a man would say, "Ah, who cares? They're all a bunch of crooks." It did their hearts good to remember him.

But all the same he told the fellows to lay off the joke when his son was around. And one day several weeks later when he was having lunch with his wife and his son, he turned to his wife and said, "You remember that Turk who stayed with us in London? I got a letter from him the other day. He wanted us to know he's doing wonderfully. He moved to Greece, and he opened up the best Turkish restaurant in Greece. He said everything is going wonderfully."

The boy was so happy to hear it that he had to go outside and play basketball.

"And he still hasn't forgotten about Egypt, I suppose," the boy's mother said.

"No, he has not."

THE BOOK THAT WAS TOO GOOD TO READ

There was an Iranian family. They were in America. None of them knew what that meant. They were not dreamy about America. They were dreamy about other things. They were so dreamy about them that they did not talk about them very much. They did not say the words "love" and "justice" and "peace" very often because their dreaming was constant. It was the sunlight that ran through their house in summer and the darkness that ran through it in winter.

The boy wanted to be a writer. He believed that being a writer had something to do with love and justice and peace, but he did not yet know how. One day in summer, he picked up a book called Division Street: America, by a man named Studs Terkel. It was an oral history—people talking about their lives in Chicago. He read the first fifty pages, and then he put down the book and went downstairs and told his family, "I think I know what America is."

"What?" they said.

"It is people."

They were quiet. They knew he was right. Okay, they thought, now what? The boy went upstairs to read again.

He had never had a book do to him what the book was doing to him. It was telling him that there was art in the lives of people. And it was doing it without a writer. If this is how it is, he thought, think of what a writer can do. Think of what a writer can do if he is as honest as a tape recorder. It was frightening, in a good way, to think that something so magnificent could be so easy. And he focused on the sun and the warm air and the smell of bark outside in order to remember that a lot of magnificent things were easy.

The sun and the warm air and the bark were American, and if he were speaking in an oral history, he would describe them honestly and how they had helped him.

This is too much, he thought.

He went back downstairs. "Don't let me read any more of that book," he said to his little sister.

"What book?"

"The oral history."

"Why not?"

"It is making me want to be an oral historian."

"What is that?"

"It is somebody who listens to people's stories and writes them down."

"That sounds wonderful. What is wrong with that?"

"I am a writer. When you see me going upstairs, say 'Don't read that book.'"

"Why don't you just take the book out of your room?"

"Because maybe I am wrong. Maybe it is exactly what I should be reading. It is too good," he said.

His sister turned back to the television. The boy walked back upstairs.

"Don't read the book," she called.

"What do you know?" he said, quietly enough that she wouldn't hear him.

Upstairs in his room he looked at the book on his desk. Are you trying to tell me that all people have to do is tell me their story and I love them, he thought, even if their story has all kinds of foolishness in it. Are you trying to tell me that it is really going to be that easy to be American? Just listen? That's all? Good Lord, that's what I've been wanting to do in the first place.

Let me read a few more pages, he thought, just to be sure.

The boy read the next fifty pages, full of the lives of people who would not go down in history unless the definition of history were to change. He hoped he could change it. That was all he wanted to do as a writer—change the definition of history so that it included everybody, everybody who had been excluded up till now.

I have to start with either everybody, he thought, or just me.

The oral history made him think that he should start with everybody, and then he would lose himself a little because he was only one page of that book, and why should he think that he was a whole book by himself?

Okay, he thought, that's it.

He went downstairs and gave the book to his sister.

"Take it," he said. "Take it and hide it somewhere I can't find it."

"Okay," she said. She took it and sat with it as she watched television.

"Well?" he asked.

"I am watching a show."

"A show?" he said. "I am talking about life."

"I'll hide it when the commercial comes."

The boy paced around the room. It was insulting to have to wait for a commercial before his sister would hide a book that needed to be hidden so badly.

Their father came into the room. "Why are you walking like that?"

"I need Leila to hide a book, but she is watching television."

"Is it a bad book?"

"No, it is a very good book."

"It is too good," the girl said. She made a face to suggest that not a hint of mockery was in her words.

"I feel sorry for you," the boy said. "I feel sorry for you if you don't know what it's like when a book is too good to read."

"I don't know what it's like when a book is too good to read," their father said. "I don't mind if you feel sorry for *me*. I felt sorry for my father too. Do you know why I felt sorry for him?"

The children were quiet, even though they knew.

"He couldn't read," their father said.

They were glad they hadn't said anything, because their father was very good at feeling sorry. Something in the way he said it made the boy think of the oral history. It was something about telling another's story the way he or she would tell it. The boy had thought for a long time that art lay in telling everyone else's story in *his* way, because he had a lot to say about people and because they didn't seem to be paying attention to their lives as stories. And they were American, so they were always rushing around doing things and going to the next place, while he was still thinking about the last one. It hadn't seemed strange to him at all that an Iranian boy would be the one to tell their story. He was already comfortable with sitting still.

The oral history made him feel like they *were* paying attention to it. They just needed someone to believe that their paying attention meant something. It was a lot to ask, but it was exactly what he wanted to do.

I shouldn't be afraid of the oral history, he thought. I shouldn't be afraid of the feeling of wanting to be an oral historian. I shouldn't be afraid of something that is very close to what I want to do, only a little different.

"I'll take the book," the boy said, tiredly and burdenedly.

"You're just going to come back down telling me to get rid of it," his sister said.

"No," he said, "I won't. I promise."

"What is the book about?" their father asked.

"It is about everybody."

"Everybody?" their father asked. "Am I in there?"

"Yes," the boy said, thinking of the strikers and organizers. "Who you would be if you had grown up in America is in it."

The father smiled. My boy is crazy, he thought.

"I don't know what to do with it," the boy said. "I don't know if I should leave for Chicago or if I should talk to everyone in our neighborhood or if I should sit down and write about myself for hours."

"It must be a good book."

The boy looked at his sister, but she didn't say it. She knew when something wasn't something to joke about anymore.

"Well, you are in America," their father said. "You have grown up here. It is good to find out about the lives of the people here."

"I just wish I knew if I was learning it from the inside or the outside," the boy said. "I feel like it is from the inside when I am reading it. But I don't know."

"You should believe it is from the inside. You should believe it is from the inside when it comes to people."

The boy wished he could explain to his father: It's not just the poor ones. It's not just the factory workers and the teachers and the communists. I love them, but what are you supposed to do when a book has everybody? What are you supposed to do when a book is so good that the writer disappears? I don't know if I should disappear or appear as much as possible. I don't want to think that those are the only two choices.

He wished he could explain to his father that maybe in Iran the factory workers and teachers and communists would've been enough, but when you didn't know the people, your only chance was with everybody. Your only chance was to listen to all of them, and maybe he was scared of how easy that was in a book because he didn't know what that would look like in life. He didn't know if an old woman would be as likely to tell him about her life growing up in Chicago in life, but he did think that he would be as likely to want to hear it. It was all an effort to figure out where he was. Her childhood in Chicago was very important to understanding where he was.

But still, he felt glad that his father had told him to believe that he was learning from the inside. It did *feel* that way when he read the oral history, whether or not he knew anything about Chicago and its neighborhoods and its past. What it was saying was something he had been suspecting: that everybody was a genius at his or her own life—each one really was—and as long as that was the case, he had a place among the people; his family had a place among them too; there was genius in living, and there was genius in living with a consideration all the time of love and justice and peace, and everybody's life belonged in an oral history, and he could live in a way that showed that truth.

He took the book and began walking upstairs.

"Can I read it when you're done?" his sister asked.

"Sure," he said, "I'll put it in your room."

"Thanks," she said.

"You can let me know if it turns out to be too good, and I'll hide it for you."

"Okay," she said, and she pretended like there was a chance of that happening, and the boy pretended like he couldn't tell.

THE FLANNERY O'CONNOR AWARD
FOR SHORT FICTION

David Walton, *Evening Out*

Leigh Allison Wilson, *From the Bottom Up*

Sandra Thompson, *Close-Ups*

Susan Neville, *The Invention of Flight*

Mary Hood, *How Far She Went*

François Camoin, *Why Men Are Afraid of Women*

Molly Giles, *Rough Translations*

Daniel Curley, *Living with Snakes*

Peter Meinke, *The Piano Tuner*

Tony Ardizzone, *The Evening News*

Salvatore La Puma, *The Boys of Bensonhurst*

Melissa Pritchard, *Spirit Seizures*

Philip F. Deaver, *Silent Retreats*

Gail Galloway Adams, *The Purchase of Order*

Carole L. Glickfeld, *Useful Gifts*

Antonya Nelson, *The Expendables*

Nancy Zafris, *The People I Know*

Debra Monroe, *The Source of Trouble*

Robert H. Abel, *Ghost Traps*

T. M. McNally, *Low Flying Aircraft*

Alfred DePew, *The Melancholy of Departure*

Dennis Hathaway, *The Consequences of Desire*

Rita Ciresi, *Mother Rocket*

Dianne Nelson, *A Brief History of Male Nudes in America*

Christopher McIlroy, *All My Relations*

Alyce Miller, *The Nature of Longing*

Carol Lee Lorenzo, *Nervous Dancer*

C. M. Mayo, *Sky over El Nido*

Wendy Brenner, *Large Animals in Everyday Life*

Paul Rawlins, *No Lie Like Love*

Harvey Grossinger, *The Quarry*

Ha Jin, *Under the Red Flag*

Andy Plattner, *Winter Money*

Frank Soos, *Unified Field Theory*

Mary Clyde, *Survival Rates*